MONICA NEVER SHUTS UP

12 stories by

A.S. KING

Cover design by A.S. King
Interior design by Caryatid Design

Earlier versions of the following stories appeared in the following magazines: "Monica Never Shuts Up," *Washington Square;* "Can You See Lois Gardening?" *Amarillo Bay;* "River 16," *Eclectica;* "Skin," *Underground Voices;* "Raul Shows Me Things," *Word Riot;* "I Am Mommy," *Literary Mama;* "Harry's Giant," *Eclectica;* "Leroy Can Tell You When," *frigg,* 2008; "How I Became My Father," *Lit103.3;* "Will Deirdre Beat The Odds?" *Contrary;* "The Tests I Failed," *Quality Women's Fiction.*

ACKNOWLEDGEMENTS

Thanks are due.

To Sara J. Henry for her keen eye and EJ Knapp for his mad skills and to both of them for their longtime friendship.

To the Backspace story contests, which got me writing shorts again after a ten year break, and to Mark Bastable and Keith Cronin whose feedback and support was invaluable.

To the many magazine and journal editors who published these stories in the first place.

To my friends, family and fans. Three F words I adore the most.

MONICA NEVER SHUTS UP

Monica never shuts up. And everything she says is utter bullshit. My brother must be thinking with his dick again. I want to strangle her before she marries him, ruins him, and steals his inheritance.

I promised our mother I'd take care of him. He was seventeen at her funeral, fifteen at Dad's. I was his guardian until graduation. I drove him back and forth to college, taught him how to make macaroni and cheese. I tried to teach him about women and I thought with that big brain of his, he'd be able to spot a gold-digging slut a light-year away.

Of course, his brain isn't half as big as he thinks it is. I mean, I love him and he's smart, yes, but book-smart. Marrying this girl is the dumbest move he's ever made. It's one thing if she hides it—if she's sweet and competent, if she's a down-home good girl to begin with. Even smart people get fooled, right? But this chick—she's a train wreck. And she never shuts up, so there's plenty of real-time evidence to support my argument. Only no one else cares.

The line I'm walking is getting shaky. Which one would my mother want? Would she want me to take care of Scott by telling him his fiancée is a loser? Or would she want me to take care of Scott by supporting even his stupidest mistakes?

I invite them to dinner on my moral tightrope.

The three of us are balancing, eating a salad.

"I can't have dressing with sugar in it. I'm diabetic," she says, gulping at a glass of Coke.

"I have a severe allergy to mushrooms," she says, eating my homemade soup, unaware that there are mushrooms in it. "I'd die instantly if I ate even one mush-room."

Really? Good. Then die instantly. That will save us all a bunch of trouble.

Fill in the blank. Monica has met _____.
    a. Marilyn Manson.
    b. Eminem.
    c. Johnny Depp.
    d. Whoever you are talking about right now.
    e. All of the above.

"Yeah. And then we all went partying at a local club. It was cool," she says.

So, apparently, my brother is unaware that he is screwing an emotional ten-year-old. No one has told him that he is now a brain-pedophile. Something must have happened to this girl to make her so twisted-dumb. She's so twisted-dumb she thinks I buy this crap.

"Don't you just love her?" Scott asks me.

"If you do, I do, I guess."

He's looking at me in that way—half amused, half confused—when she comes back from the bathroom. "That's a great print you have in the bathroom, Sadie. You know, I met Keith Haring once."

I'm doing the math. Keith Haring died when Monica was eight.

"Really? Where?" I ask.

"I was working in New York, you know, modeling. He came into a shoot."

Scott sits up. "You were a model in New York?" he says.

I can see Scott's dick smiling. It loves that Scott is screwing a New York model.

"Mmm-hmm. That's how I worked my way through college."

"Keith Haring came to a shoot you were doing? What year was that?" I ask.

2

"Ninety-four."

"You were thirteen?"

"Yeah."

I can see her internally counting fingers from my high wire.

"Keith Haring died in nineteen-ninety," I say.

"Did he?"

Scott moves toward her and rubs her arm sympathetically. He is engaged to the infirm. He's marrying mental cancer. "So you were modeling in New York when you were eight? Wow. That must have been cool."

"Yeah. It was."

Multiple choice. Monica, in her twenty-four years on Earth, has:

    a. Been a New York supermodel.

    b. Lived in the "ghetto" dealing and doing every drug known to man.

    c. Partied with whoever you are talking about right now.

    d. Earned two college degrees and worked professionally in over ten fields of expertise.

    e. Somehow banged my brother into a big enough idiot that he proposed to her.

    f. All of the above.

We're in the hallway, alone. She confides in me. "I had sex with the bass player from Soundgarden once, and afterward, he asked me to come on tour with them."

> > >

She's walking down the aisle. I can see the outline of her nipple rings through the wedding dress. I am in a church, praying to God that my mother isn't watching this spectacle.

Everything is muffled.

I imagine myself standing up. I hear myself saying,

"She's not good enough for my brother." I see a church full of their cyber-freak-friends staring at me. Blink. My mother is talking to me. She's sitting at the piano in the front of the church. *You have to let the girl trip herself up, Sadie. Give her enough rope.*

Outside the church, I throw bridal birdseed at her with such force, welts raise on her arm. I throw another handful at her face. A seed is stuck in her eye. She stops halfway down the steps and picks it out. My brother looks around while I duck behind the crowd of rowdy misfits and sneak off to my car.

At the reception, Monica's mother is standing three steps from the bar, chewing on a spinach and feta cheese cracker. She's wearing a classy mauve dress that matches the balloons swaying above every table. I've only met her once before, at the wedding shower, where we managed to gingerly skim the details of my parents' deaths before she had better things to do.

"It must have been tough dealing with all of her illnesses," I say, even though I know this isn't the time or place for my investigation.

"I'm sorry. I don't know what you mean."

"The diabetes, you know. The allergies and stuff."

"Monica isn't diabetic."

"Oh. I must have mixed that up," I say.

"She was always a healthy girl."

"I guess she'd have to be to get all that modeling work when she was so young."

"What?"

"The modeling work. In New York. You know."

"I'm sorry. I need to refill my drink."

I'm at the head table, standing while people tap on their glasses with their forks to get Monica and Scott to kiss each other. I wait until they're done with an especially inappropriate and long tongue-kiss before I start my unrehearsed speech. I've had three hot brandies. "Since

4

our parents can't be here," I start, "I wanted to say a few words on this special day.

"Ever since Scott was a little kid, he'd steal my magazines to look at the models." There's a chuckle from the audience. "I can't tell you how amazing it is that he found Monica—a real live supermodel—and fell in love. This is a dream come true. I am sure our parents are looking down this very minute and are so proud to have such a prestigious daughter-in-law." I make a motion as if to toast, and the room toasts and drinks with me.

Her side of the family looks perplexed. I look at Scott. He still has absolutely no idea that he has married an imposter.

Six months later. We're eating dinner at my place. I have laced every course with hidden mushrooms. She still won't die. I think Scott is starting to doubt her now. He told me on the phone last week that she wouldn't show him any of the magazine covers she posed for. She said she was too shy to show him. She said she burnt them all after a phase of overwhelming modesty during her senior year in college. He said he was going to start looking for copies at the library, which, to me, sounds like he's starting to wonder. So, at dinner, I ask her about the good old days in the big apple.

Multiple choice. Monica never *said* she was a model. What she *said* was:

    a. She was doing a project for school about modeling.
    b. She was researching careers and thought she might want to be a photographer.
    c. She was *thinking* about it, but decided not to.
    d. "They" called, asking her to model, but her mother made her say no.
    e. All of the above.

To change the subject, she says, "Sadie, this place could really use some interior design touches. I have a degree in that, you know. Well, not like they ever bothered to send me the piece of paper, but I did plenty of classes. I designed the lobby of the Marriott in New York and a bunch of other big places."

I ignore her offer to redesign my house and move on to dessert.

Halfway through a double-sized piece of mushroom/fudge cake I ask her how she manages to balance her sugar, being diabetic and all.

"I'm type five."

"What?"

"She's type five," Scott says, annoyed.

"Oh. I never heard of that one. What does it do to you?"

"It means I can have all the sugar I want, as long as I don't get fat."

Oh God. My brother is so freaking stupid.

Six months later, I get the invitation to the anniversary party, and I decide not to RSVP. Fuck her. She has stolen my only sibling and made him into an accomplice. He is the same fraud she is now.

He called me two weeks ago, angry.

"Why did you tell Monica that her taste in decorating was bad?"

"I never said that. I haven't talked to Monica in months."

"She says you called."

"I didn't call."

"Well, you shouldn't be so rude."

"I wasn't."

"She said you were."

"I wasn't. I haven't talked to her since you guys were here for dinner."

"Are you saying she's lying?"

6

"Isn't she always?"

"What?" It was like Scott lowered fifty of those city-proof steel shutters at once. I could feel it over the phone line. Either he's in denial or he's the dimmest man on planet Earth.

"Nothing. Forget it."

Fill in the blank. Monica told my brother that _____
   a. She turned down three real jobs to make time for decorating my place.
   b. She sent me a job quote and a consultation invoice which I refuse to pay.
   c. My lack of payment has freaked her out so much, she needs two massages a week at fifty bucks a pop.
   d. I am the reason she's too stressed to conceive.
   e. All of the above.

I make a raspberry/mushroom torte. I make a pecan/mushroom pie. I have dried and ground a half pound of the fuckers and have them in a black Kodak film container in my purse to sprinkle on every hors d'oeuvre I can find because this has become the only way I can deal with Monica. Pretending to poison her is my coping skill—it makes me feel like I'm doing *something*.

I approach her acne-scarred sister Darla, whom I spoke to briefly at their wedding, and who is the only person in the room not ignoring me.

"A year already," I say.

"Yep."

"Time flies."

"Yep."

I squint to remember the details from our chat a year before. "You're a psychologist, right?"

"Yep," she says, "Ironic, isn't it?"

"I'm sorry. I don't follow."

"Oh, you know. I'm a shrink and my sister is so screwed up."

I think my jaw is hanging open. I reach my right hand up and hinge it shut. "Screwed up?" I say, giving her a second to explain, which she doesn't. "You mean the stories?"

"That's a nice way of saying it." She slurps back some Diet 7-Up and smacks her lips.

I nod and offer her some of my torte.

"She's been at it since she could talk. Youngest. Always needed attention," she says, with too big a mouthful of raspberries. "Moved schools every year or two, once the other kids figured her out. Never had a friend for more than a few months at a stretch. Honestly, I can't believe your brother is sticking it out so long."

"Yeah. Me neither, I guess." Suddenly, I feel bad for Monica. And in that sympathy, I see why Scott is sticking it out, but I continue with my investigation, because Darla seems to be the only person I will ever get the truth from. "Scott says getting married has really boosted her confidence and has helped her stay clean."

"Clean?" she cackles and slaps her thigh, "Good Lord! That's *me*. *I'm* the addict in the family! Monica wouldn't know a drug if it bit her on the ass! God! That girl! I don't know why – but for her whole life, she's wanted to be me. And look! Look!" She holds her arms out, posing. "Who the hell would want to be this fat mess?"

I can't nod to that, but I see her point and slide another serving of torte onto the black plastic plate.

"She tells people she's a psychologist all the time. When I took a class in decorating, she started telling people she was an interior designer. She even says she's diabetic, but not 'fat diabetic' like me."

"She's not diabetic?" I don't know why I'm asking this. I know damn well she isn't.

"Hell no. And she was never an alcoholic and she isn't allergic to eggs or mayonnaise or mushrooms or nuts either. All me."

I stare at her and let the sentence catch up with me.

"You're allergic to mushrooms?"

She chews and washes the bite back with more Diet 7-Up. "Yep. And for the record, I don't believe a word she says about you."

"Uh," I struggle. "How allergic to mushrooms are you?"

She's looking across the room at three pierced Goth-freaks who've just come in and doesn't see how serious my face is. "Well, the last time I ate some, I was in the hospital an hour later in anaphylactic shock. Why?"

Before I can answer, I hear Monica screaming from the kitchen.

"Mushrooms? *Mushrooms*? Aunt Kate! I'm *allergic* to mushrooms!"

Scott runs by me and grabs the phone out of its cradle. He dials 911.

Monica's crying now. "I could *DIE*!"

Darla rolls her eyes at me, "Here we go again."

The ambulance lights are drawing a crowd on their small town street. She's crying-yelling from the stretcher, "Scott! *SCOTT*! Where are you, Scott?" He's in here, leaned down to my lips. I'm telling him my year-long secret. I hand him the film container full of mushroom dust. I tell him she's a lying simpleton. That I hate her. That I knew from the day I met her that she was a gold-digging loser. I tell him that we have to get Darla into the ambulance because she *really is* allergic to mushrooms and could croak at any minute. After staring at his shoes for a second, he looks at me over his vintage horn-rims. He knows. And now he knows I know, too.

Aunt Kate is bawling with guilt in the living room. She truly thinks that her chicken vol-au-vents with a light mushroom sauce might kill her niece tonight. Darla is kneeling next to the sofa, trying to calm her down when Scott whispers something to her.

"Been there, done that, Scott. You're her husband. You

can handle it."

"Yeah, but you're her sister and know all about her *medical history*," he says through clenched teeth, finally allowing the anger to hit him.

Darla puts a chubby hand on her hip. "That's easy. Nothing's wrong with her. That's her medical history."

To my relief, Scott is nodding. "Yes. But you're a *psychologist.*" To this, Darla sighs knowingly, shakes her head, and starts to get up. Then, she sports a puzzled brow. Coughs. Coughs again. Coughs again. The wheezing starts. Then, she promptly falls over and begins convulsing right at Aunt Kate's feet, who screams, "Oh my God! I've killed them both!"

Fill in the blank. Before the ink on their divorce is dry, Monica _____.

    a. Hired a TV lawyer to sue me for a job she never did on my house.

    b. Told Scott she never loved him and that his breath always stinks.

    c. Got knocked up by the lead singer from Alice in Chains.

    d. Started dating that guy with the tongue stud who works at the pet store.

    e. All of the above.

Multiple choice. Of all the things I learned this year, the most important was:

    a. Scott can take care of his own problems.

    b. Spiking food with allergens is not a clever coping skill.

    c. We are all, essentially, on our own in this world.

    d. I need more excitement in my life.

    e. All of the above.

Can You See Lois Gardening?

What harm am I doing? More money than God, they have—and it's only dirt I'm taking, roots and leaves and dirt is all. I'm not in their top-drawer jewels or their Jaguar convertibles. I haven't kidnapped their daughter or dog or mother-in-law. It's simple. I just want more beauty in my life.

Caleb drives me around in his Ford pickup. He brings his Willie Nelson tapes and hums along, out of tune. He drives slow, half in the shoulder, as if he's delivering the *Merchandiser*, you know—that newspaper with things for sale cheap, so I can scope out the specimens as we go by, and if I tell him to stop, he stops and I hop out with my little shovel and dig up what I want. It's easy.

My mother used to do it with mushrooms and walnuts. She'd make us all get out of the van and collect as many as we could. She'd never ask permission. But the twelve-year-old-looking cop that came last week told me that I have to ask permission now.

To me, that's like asking permission to use a trash can on a city street.

It's like asking permission to sneeze.

The plants are growing. They need to be thinned. I am doing them a favor.

Everything was fine until the Mexican woman saw me. I bet there were plenty of other things she could have been doing other than catching me digging out her neighbor's ferns.

"Hey!"

I turned around and looked up the hill.

"What are you doing?"

I got back in the truck and Caleb peeled out, like in *The Dukes of Hazard*. But she must have got our license plate number because the blond teenager cop came later that day to Caleb's house.

I was on my knees, watering my new ferns, right next to the three new species of late-blooming lilies I got from over in the west-side suburbs. Next to that, a whole handful of mystery bulbs (flat, like buttons, but much smaller than Gladioli) that I found in the dirt I was digging around a small Japanese maple.

Caleb never likes it when I get trees. He says there's a line I'm crossing when I do that. "People pay good money for trees," he says. I say yeah—people pay good money for blow jobs, too. Doesn't mean they deserve them.

"Ma'am, I can't do much *to* you," the cop finally said, after I gave him one of my Frescas, patted him on his crew cut, and told him about my disability check not stretching like it used to. "But I *can* ask you, as an officer of the peace, to stop stealing people's plants."

He looked at my garden and back at me. He looked past me and into Caleb's stockpile of crap in the hallway, and over at Caleb, who was dove halfway into the back of an old television with a screwdriver and a flashlight. His shirt was about four days greasy and he never did put pants on anymore unless we were going out.

"Good day," the cop said, and tipped his hat, got in his squad car, and drove away. I figure he must have understood.

These are my babies. They love me and I love them. I deserve them because God took away my two boys with war. I deserve them because God took away my first husband with cancer and my mother and father with heart disease. I deserve them because I have nothing else. Not one inch of dirt. Not one blade of grass. Not one grain of food. All I have is Caleb's place. And he lets me plant it up and take care of it even though we're divorced going on two years.

> > >

Fact is, I couldn't kick her out if I wanted to. I can't barely feed myself and the cats and dogs need tending. I only divorced her because she nagged me to do it. She said it was in my best interest, but I don't think she knows what that really means. Best interest. As if it's in someone's best interest to have their gardens dug up by a crazy loon.

I knew she didn't have nowhere to go, so I assumed she'd stay with me for a while, anyway. She's got rights, she tells me now—rights to stay, and even though I know she's full of it, I let her stay. She feeds us all and she plants up my yard with all those dug-up plants. She has it looking real pretty, too. I'm glad God gave her a thing, because in the two decades I known her, I learned she wasn't much good at nothing else.

When the cop came out because of the ferns, that's when I knew she really was crazy. She denied the whole thing, up and down. Said she never known anything about no ferns, right there, on her knees, holding the damn things. Then she crept over to the front door, to where he was, tiptoeing as if he couldn't see her. Up until then, I thought she was just being kooky, I guess. My mother used to be kooky sometimes. About four times a year, she'd turn up her Johnny Cash records and dance with me and my brother and sing loud and drink bourbon.

So I thought Lois was doing that thing. She'd drink all different concoctions and ask, "Can you see me?" and I'd say no and pretend I couldn't. You know, come to think of it, she'd ask me about three times a week. A lot more kooky than my mother ever was. And really, who, in their right mind, thinks they is invisible for *real*?

She calls it hunting and gathering. Like the old days.

She says I'm a caveman anyway, so I should know all about it. Says it ain't illegal because no one can see her doing it. Says it ain't stealing because those people probably won't eat all that food anyway. They got too much of everything, she says. They'll let the birds at the spaghetti squash or the berries. They'll let the rabbits eat those radishes if she don't pick them. The carrots. The lettuce. The corn on the cob will rot. The tomatoes will sour. The peas will turn to starch.

She takes two fast gulps of Fresca and thinks she's some see-through master thief when really she's an overweight nut stalking through other people's gardens in broad daylight. My Lois, gone crazy from losing, invented her own disappearing potion and believes it works.

Although, I shouldn't be surprised. When we first got married, she believed that Tic Tacs would help make her pregnant again at forty-six, even though she knew darn well I'd had the snip a decade earlier.

I'm sorting through the mountains of Caleb's stuff. Lois is up front being dramatic for the young couple who've come to view the place. The husband is asking all sorts of questions. The wife is sticking her head into each room inside, holding her breath I bet, to block out the cat piss stench, trying to imagine the house without it being crammed full of everything that's in it.

Caleb was a pack rat. Actually, pack rat is an understatement. But he was a freaking genius, man. He didn't just store shit, he knew what he was storing, knew where it was, and how much he bought it for, and how much it was worth now. Rocks, gems, crystals, jewelry, art, tools, antiques. Caleb was one of those men who got bored quick. He was like that as a kid when we were growing up, too. Always into things. Since he'd built this place, he'd sit down here on the back porch overlooking the forest, roll a fatty, and open up a book, and then another book, and then another, until he'd learned everything there was to know about a thing. Spent a week learning cacti. Built a heated greenhouse. Grew cacti. Got bored. Learned about smoking meat. Built a smokehouse. Got meat and smoked it. Got bored. You name it, he's done it: tropical fish, salt water, cichlids, coral, seahorses and turtles. Birds, snakes, iguanas. Farm animals. Computers, cameras, small motors, big motors, tractors, table saws.

So Lois told us about a year ago that we had to stop dragging Caleb to the powwows. That he was too sick. Too sick my ass. She just hated him having any fun while he had cancer. He told me once she never gave him head—not once—in their seventeen years of marriage. Talk about a killjoy.

Yesterday, she told me not to smoke joints on the deck while I help her empty the house. I told her to go ahead and call the cops. She didn't. She's as high as I am—probably too high to dial the phone. Besides, I'm nearly sixty years old. Who the fuck does she think she's bossing?

Caleb was dead inside for two days before we found him. Lois was staying with the one sister who'll still talk to her—the one who lives in Jersey. The cats had made a mess of his face trying to get him to wake up and feed them. One even nibbled his index finger. Just my *being here* requires some kind of medication. At least mine is natural. Her synthetic pharmaceutical shit isn't getting her anywhere but heaved into the back of that Subaru every twenty minutes, bawling her freaking eyes out, man.

> > >

When Bryan called me, I knew he was serious because he sounded excited.

"We found your house. Go check your email. Call me back."

15

As I waited for the computer to spit out the picture and room measurements, I tried not to get my hopes up. We've been looking for a place for two years. Oversaturated market. Prices too high. But even when we found something close, Bryan never sounded so excited.

So I called Reg. "When can you get off work and come see this place? If we see it tonight we can put an offer in and maybe get it."

"It's that good? Why's it so cheap?"

"The guy died. Something about his ex-wife needing to sell it fast."

It's perfect. I know it the minute I see it from the road. I know it the minute I see the two broken-down VW hippie vans in the driveway. I know it the minute I see the unbelievably breathtaking landscaping up the side of the mountain. Reg turns to me, in a trance, "How much again?"

"One eighty-nine. Four acres." Japanese maples, a rare dogwood, laburnums, cherries, plums, and I think that's an apricot. More bulbs that I have ever seen in one place are poking up through the bright green new spring grass. Large rocks on the steep incline are bathed in budding vines, some of which join to a trellis on the side of the house, forming a natural pergola over the walkway leading to the deck. The house itself needs lots of work (I can't see one gutter still attached) but the garden must be worth thirty grand all by itself.

"God, Reg. I love it." I say, not even three steps into what smells like a giant litter box. We hold our breath and walk through the catacomb maze of stacked junk, peeking into the rooms. This is the house of our dreams. Modern contemporary, large lot, middle of the woods with a beautiful nearby river. Everything we ever wanted. Reg has seen enough. He's dying to talk to the seller and learn what kind of pain she's in. I tell him to go ahead, that I want another look around.

16

The seller woman is out front, using the back of her white Subaru as a chaise lounge, breathing loudly, moaning at times, guzzling at a bottle of Fresca. If I was her real estate agent, I'd have locked this woman far away from here. This house is hard enough to sell as it is. Over three-quarters full of crap, needing new sub flooring from all the pet stains, crazy-man's junkyard in the back, cascading into the woods. Upstairs rooms never drywalled or plastered. The list to do is endless. Having the *I Need Money Fast* poster woman out front, sweating and occasionally bursting into tears is not going to help increase her commission.

I can hear them talking through the open upstairs window.

She's telling him her life story between sips of Fresca.

Ex-wife. The guy left her with everything. She has to pay his overdue cancer bills with the house money. He's been dead four months now. The bill collectors are getting rough with her. Reg is saying sympathetic things. He's verbally patting her knee. He's so damn good at this.

I'm walking around the perimeter. A paper-thin half-harvested lawnmower. A stack of slates. Bricks. Cracked buckets with hardened mortar.

"Hi."

I'm startled and look up, "Hi."

"I'm Cupcake," she says. She adds, "Childhood friend."

"Oh," I say. "I'm Liz." I stretch my hand over the rotting-splintered railing. She's tapping her Birkenstock to the Credence playing on a little tape player next to her. She shakes my hand and smiles.

"These are his phone bills from 1978. When he lived in Ohio." She's got a box on her lap, filled with paper. There's a stack of these boxes behind the chair. Behind that, is a small greenhouse filled with cacti that I didn't see from the inside. And more cat shit on the floor.

Her dark, tie-dyed, jingling skirt is resting on the deck, and I can see a single knee shape poking through it. "It's a groovy place, isn't it?"

"Yeah. Do you know where the property line is?"

She points directly across a shallow gorge. Four acres of woods seems big. Cupcake says, swinging her waist-long hair over her shoulder, "Do you like it?"

"I love it. I wish I could buy it right now." I look down and sigh. "But any house we can afford, we get outbid by investors."

"Really?"

"Yeah. We've been trying for two years. Bidding fair, too."

"Fucking rich people."

"Yeah."

I wander off to finish my perimeter walk. When I get back to the Subaru, it's empty and I can hear Reg talking to the ex-wife inside the house. I peek into the garage window. The garage is filled one hundred and ten percent with junk, too.

Cupcake is walking toward me from the other side of the house. In one hand she has a thick bunch of dried sage, lit and smoking, and in the other, she's holding up what looks to be a joint. "It's my lunch break," she says, walking over to her sticker-covered van. (So one VW I included in my mental haul-away estimate is actually Cupcake's ride.) She opens the door, reaches in to grab a package of store-brand vanilla wafer cookies and a bottle of water. When she accidentally knocks the dream catcher off the rearview mirror, she leans down to pick it up and I can see she isn't wearing any underwear. Cupcake is the real deal. Straight out of 1967. "Wanna burn one?"

"Sure." This has got to be the weirdest house viewing I've ever been to. "So, are you her sister?"

"Fuck no, man! Caleb and I grew up together in Indiana. She and I never got along. Not even back when he married her.

"I'm just here to help because he would have wanted me to." She takes the joint, inserts the whole thing in her mouth, evens the spit across the paper, and then lights it. "She can't handle shit at this point."

"He seemed to be some character," I say, "I mean, he sure did know a lot of stuff about a lot of stuff."

She's nodding, holding in smoke. She hands it to me and says, "A fucking genius." I nod now, holding in smoke, too.

We do this for a minute—passing the joint back and forth—without saying anything. And then a truck slows down on the road. Stops. Turns left into the driveway. The truck reads: *DeForillo Construction.* Cupcake shakes her sage at the sky while the driver parks the truck and gets out.

She hands me the joint and walks toward him. "Where's your agent?"

"I—"

"We won't sell to investors."

"I—"

"The house is already sold. Go away," she says, now blocking him. He cocks his head, then laughs a little and gets back into his truck and leaves. The listing agent, who, up until now was gabbing on her phone in her car, gives Cupcake a look and wags her finger to scold her. Cupcake says, "What can I do?"

She walks back behind her van and I give her the joint.

"I can't guarantee we'll make a great offer or anything," I say. "It needs a lot of work. We only have so much money."

"She'll take anything. She's crazy anyway. Did you notice?"

I'm holding in smoke, but Cupcake makes me laugh through my nose. "Yeah. I noticed."

"See all these trees and flowers?" She acknowledges the landscaping.

"Mmm-hmm."

"She stole them. Right out of other people's lawns."

I look at the acre's worth of plants so artfully placed among the rocks and older trees behind the driveway. Only now do I see that the entire forest floor is pushing up dark green sprouts, too. Tens of thousands of them. The place must be worth twenty thousand in bulbs alone.

"She stole them?"

"Yep. Every single one."

"Huh." I can't believe it. It's too professional-looking for it to be made of stolen parts. Too perfect. Too like the gardens from a European movie.

"Caleb told me once that she thinks if she drinks enough Fresca, she'll become invisible."

"Hm," I manage, too stoned to even register the word *invisible*. This is definitely the weirdest house viewing I've ever been to.

Reg is saying something about replacing the sub flooring. I hear the ex-wife light one of the no-brand menthol cigarettes that were sitting outside the front door.

I hear her say, "My problem is having it emptied out before settlement. We've been here for a month already." She motions toward the house as if to say, 'See? See the goddamn mess he left me with?'

"We can do just about anything to help you, Lois," Reg says. "If you want, we can make the contract say that you get the money sooner, but you have an extra month or two to clean it out." That's my Reg. Smooth. He'll offer to help next. He'll take her out to lunch. He'll buy her a goddamned years' worth of filet mignon if he has to.

Cupcake and I come out from behind the van. Reg looks perplexed, and Lois looks pissed. Cupcake gives her a sarcastic smirk and walks back to her chair on the back deck overlooking the forest. Lois cracks open another Fresca and sits into the tailgate.

Reg and I are standing by our car.

I'm listening to his list of cost-effective upgrades. Re-

20

placing and sealing the floors, plastering the upstairs, the second floor bathroom and the shower in the master bedroom bath. Insulation, gutters, boiler service, new water heater. Three hornets' nests. Junk hauling.

"I'd bid asking price," he says.

"We'll never get it for that. Four acres? This school district?"

"We can't bid more."

He's right. We can't.

I decide to say goodbye to Cupcake while Reg has one last chat with the listing agent, who's whispering complaints about Lois into her cell phone by the garage door.

Cupcake stops sorting old mail and grins.

"You're gonna bid?"

I nod. "I hope we get it."

"I'll make sure she picks you," she says.

"Whatever. She's got to take the best offer. May the best man win, you know?"

"I'll make sure," she says, waving goodbye as I round the corner.

To my right, the landscaping reminds me who's making the decisions around here. Cupcake turns up Credence behind me and I stand under the vined pergola spying on Lois in the back of her Subaru. She's gulping, letting the fizz invade her nose, trickle down her chin, wet her t-shirt. She turns and centers herself with the rearview mirror and winces. She finds her reflection in the tinted hatchback glass, and throws the bottle toward the road. She yells something and then buries her sobbing head into her hands.

I don't hold my hopes high for us getting this house.

On signing day, I bring Lois a case of Fresca and a box of assorted gladiola bulbs that I bought on sale at the dollar store. She says thank you, but doesn't make eye contact. She brought Cupcake, who hugs me warmly and says nice things. *I didn't think I'd see you again! I'm so glad you got it.* I didn't know she would be here, and I feel bad for not bringing her anything, though I'm not sure what I'd give Cupcake if I had the chance.

I don't think she needs anything.

I think about this as we sign the papers and pass pens and contracts around the table. *I don't think she needs anything.* I look at the two of them, Cupcake and Lois, and I realize that I am sitting at a table with two examples of what my life can come to. Reg and I are young. This is our first house. We are beginning. We have a choice.

When the meeting is over, Lois simply walks out. Cupcake stops to hug Reg and me and wish us good luck. I make a mental note. It says: *Choose to be free.*

I Am Mommy

Act One

Mommy has locked herself down in the basement. She is tired of the world, so she twisted the latch and stole her life back. Just for a minute.

Mommy has a phone down there. She is calling her friends. Chatting. Shooting the shit. She is giving her nursing breasts a rest. She is breathing. Blinking. Thinking. She is not thinking about anyone's overdue library book. Or their silver hair clip or sweat socks. She is not scouring the stain from a brand new ten-dollar t-shirt or calculating the time since the baby's last feed. She is not calling the guidance counselor, the hockey coach, or the school nurse.

She is calling her mother. She is calling to explain that she understands now.

She understands now.

"Mom, I understand why you locked yourself in the basement," she says. "It's so quiet."

Mommy is lucky. She has a washing machine down there. And a dryer. She has a sink to wash her teeth in if she's gutsy enough to use one of the old toothbrushes that she collects for scrubbing the grooves in blackened silver. She has a dehumidifier, so she'll never feel damp, and a boiler so she'll never get cold.

All her mother had was a coal bin and a shovel. Mousetraps, a rusty clothes-wringer and dust. (All her mother's mother had was buried pennies in the dirt floor, away from that drunken slob of a son.)

"I'm so sorry," Mommy says to her mother. "I wish I would have been a better kid.

"The time I stole forty dollars out of your wallet. The tantrums I'd throw when you had to go to work. The charge card incident.

"How can I make it up to you?"

ACT TWO

Mommy is back from the nursing home and her eyes are wet. She files the day's foreclosure notice with the other three, right next to a brightly colored pamphlet about how to survive bankruptcy. Someone screams about the permission slip she never signed and returned. Someone else can't find their shoes. Mommy sits on the tartan swivel chair and looks at her watch.

Then she drags herself to the closet in her bedroom to get dressed for work.

She has a phone up there, and it rings. And it's the administrator/charge nurse/billing clerk. It's the doctor/surgeon/occupational therapist. It's her mother again.

"I'm doing the best I can," Mommy says to her mother, "but it's never enough."

Mommy has locked herself in the basement again. She's packing the few things she has left and is throwing everything else away. She's yelling and crying and won't answer the phone. She's karate-chopping the appliances, boxing the water heater, fiberglass insulation cushioning her red knuckles. She is ignoring the flower delivery and the sympathy cards. She is considering burning them with the nursing home bills. Or burning down the whole damn billing department—who charged two bucks per diaper when her mother ran out. A dollar-fifty for a Tylenol or a Band-Aid while her children ate cheese

24

sandwiches again, with ice water, for Sunday dinner.

Don't worry. She's not sick or too far gone. She doesn't require medication/hospitalization/tough love. She knows her life isn't a waste. (It's only money.)

ACT THREE

Mommy's children visit her five-story apartment complex in town to make sure she's taking her protein supplements and extra calcium. They take her for walks on evenly paved paths and ask the hairdresser for "something easy to take care of." She's not a bother or a pest. She is atoning for not being able to pay for college. For never affording the wedding reception/dress/tuxedo rental. She is cashing in her life's rain check gracefully, without too much expectation. She knows the children talk. About her. About what to do.

"Please don't ever send me there," Mommy says. Anywhere but there.

Anywhere but there.

"You don't understand," she says. "That place swallowed my life."

> > >

Mommy plays bingo in the rec room with the others. Last time she overheard, she was doing well in her new environment. The nurses don't say anything directly, except when they want her to move.

"Dinnertime!"

"It's time for our walk!"

"Are you ready for activities?"

"Groovy Granny exercise!"

They're always smiling. Like clowns.

Last time she overheard, it was costing a fortune. The insurance is all messed up. Medicare doesn't buy what it used to. Mommy's son-in-law is beginning to look like a human calculator. And tired. They all look so tired.

They put her in rubber pants again. Mommy hates rubber pants. But the human calculator can't afford enough store-brand Depends, and the new pills the doctor prescribed are making her go twice as much so she leaves a trail of liquid behind her wherever she sits. Mommy heard the nurses make a joke. They call her "The Snail."

Mommy, AKA "The Snail" is learning Transcendental Meditation. The Groovy Granny exercise lady has a class every Monday and Friday in the rec room. Mommy is sitting with her back straight, breathing, and clearing her mind. She is creating her sanctuary.

"Your sanctuary can be anywhere you feel most comfortable," she hears. "Somewhere pleasant and peaceful."

She flies out the window, up to the clouds above her old neighborhood, and down, into her old house—the house the bank finally took. She flies into the basement and sees they've managed all this time with the same old water heater, still wrapped in a red fiberglass cozy. Mommy marvels how the old appliance will outlive her.

Then, she pictures herself sitting in lotus position on the basement floor. She pictures her hands folded calmly in her lap. She pictures a gasoline can. A match. Just like Thich Quang Duc in 1963 protesting in Vietnam. She is at peace, burning. The house/herself/the water heater. She is finally fighting back.

Her burning is cut short by the instructor's hand on her arm.

"Of course I'm all right," she says. "I was just transcending. Isn't that what I'm supposed to do?"

> > >

Mommy has been moved to a different room. She has to share now, with a roommate. They have a phone that doesn't dial out and never rings except for telemarketers. Last time she overheard, the billing department was sick of chasing up money, of bouncing checks and maxed credit cards. Mommy thinks this generation has it harder than she ever did. To live now is to always be digging.

It's Friday and Mommy has a visitor. A grandchild, sweet smelling and soft, spitting up curdled milk and mucus on everyone's shoulder. This is what it's all about. Babies making babies making babies. And now Mommy is the calculator's baby, when he should be enjoying his newfound fatherhood, not bouncing checks for the sake of a hot meal three times a day topped with tapioca pudding.

During meditation class, Mommy flies to the parking lot and siphons gas from a sky-blue Chrysler LeBaron into the clear quart bottle they gave her to pee in. She fastens the cap and hides it under her chair. She flies to the nurses' lunchroom and steals matches from nurse Fran's coat pocket.

After class, Mommy passes the dining room where some women, snackers with fat asses, are gathered eating mid-afternoon ice cream cones. She waves calmly when she passes the physical therapy room and smiles when she shuffles past the upright oak-stained piano and the war heroes who tell Korea stories on the floral couches. One of the men mumbles something about how she must be lost.

"Nothing back there but accountants and girls in suits," she hears.

Of course, she knows exactly where she's going and what she's doing. She enters the employee-only area and quickly finds the door marked *Billing*.

River 16

H-125 has one river. One polluted river. It's like wading through chest-high metal-flecked molasses, only loaded with floating industrial waste and dead people. When I work there, they pay me seven hundred Earth dollars per hour.

Other than the river, H-125 doesn't offer much by way of interesting scenery. The surface is potholed like the moon, but uglier. Half of it is covered in mines, so we can take every last ounce of aluminum ore and ship it home to Earth for just one more year of them living like a planet full of deluded assholes. The few monochromatic canyons and peaks are interesting enough, unless you've seen the Grand Canyon or the Rockies, like I have. Of course, I never will again. Even if I do make the lottery, I'll be too old to go.

I was shipped to H-125 fourteen years ago and worked in the mines at first—back-breaking prison labor—then graduated to my freedom and this job in sector 3-C sifting through the polluted River 16 to weed out bodies, refrigerators, televisions, transports, or any other things that the population here tosses in that might clog the hydro-generator. Of course, if a dead body gets to me, then Frank in sector 2-H isn't doing his job. And if a small household appliance floats this far, that means Denny in sector 2-D isn't doing his job either. I can't say I blame them, though. I used to work in sector 2 and the smell of the crematorium is enough to make you pass out sometimes. Plus Denny and Frank, like most of us, are crippled after working so long and hard in the mines.

The planet's population is divided now, after forty years, between prisoners who work off their crimes and don't get paid, and ex-prisoners like us, who work with industrial independent contractors for more money than we'd ever see on Earth.

The only problem with making seven hundred dollars an hour is that there is nothing on H-125 to buy. Nothing. It's a 100% free society. But they pay us anyway. So life is a constant state of economic impotence. It's like living inside of an eyeball but not being able to see out.

Here's how the math works. Seven hundred an hour is seven grand a day. That's forty-two thousand a week, which is two million one hundred thousand dollars a year. And I get to glare at it every month on payday—my balance. The balance of my life. Ten digital numbers on a screen.

My $24,864,990.11. Say it with me. Twenty-four million eight hundred and sixty-four thousand, nine hundred and ninety dollars and eleven cents. I can't send it home and I can't buy anything with it. Unless I win the lottery in the next seven months, my time is up. My imaginary money comes with me down River 16, the waterway of the euthanized, to be plucked out by Frank or whoever replaces me in section 3-C, and reduced to ash the color of an H-125 sunrise. The few who make the lottery before they reach age fifty are allowed to transfer their credits earned here to a bank on Earth and return home, but unless you get lucky, all you have is a number on a screen to look at until they retire you.

Back home, I used to fish on the Niagara River when I was a boy. The Earth Corps had restored it in the twenty-third century after centuries of abuse and neglect. They paid for projects like river restoration and oceanic filters and arctic ice cleanings by discovering and mining distant planets filled with what Earth consumers were

29

still buying. Like some bum at the turn of the millennium, they were trading soda cans for nickels, and using the nickels to pay for more soda cans.

I grew up and had a beautiful family. Two boys, a baby girl, and Jean, my soulmate wife. We lived in a small, solar-heated home on the east side of Rochester, in a community known for its low population, which, when I was sent away, was around two million people. The rest of New York state wasn't so lucky. When Manhattan sank, the thirty million survivors scattered to the most nearby places. Lust for higher ground crowded the Catskill, the Pocono, and the Adirondack Mountains. Rochester, being lakeside, was spared too much of an influx.

I was never any good at history, but from what I remember, recycling laws came into effect in the USA sometime in the twenty-first century. After the second revolution in 2234, the laws went lax for a while, but by the time my eldest boy Ginero was born one hundred years later, the squads were out in full force every waste collection day, with their detectors and their electronic citation devices. Until Ginero became a teenager, we never got a fine.

Two soda cans in the regular paper/composting trash cost me four thousand five hundred dollars. Five weeks later, Jean mustn't have been paying attention one day and threw a glass jar in the wrong bin and that cost me a second fine, which was double the first, and a strict warning that the limit was five. Five fines, and then prison for the homeowner. This was the twenty-fourth century—mistakes of this sort would not be tolerated.

I held a family meeting explaining that if we weren't careful, they could put me in jail, and so, we would no longer be buying anything in glass jars or cans, and every bag of trash that went from the kitchen to the garage would be inspected by me from now on. At that, Ginero tried every single day to slip something in past my eyes.

It was his teenaged way of pressing authority, I suppose, but he didn't understand the consequences. I would lose my job at the advertising firm. I would go to jail. Our family's upper-middle class existence would disappear so quickly that soon we would be no different from the riffraff that settled in the mountaintop cities of New Harlem or New Brooklyn or New Bronx. Ginero was thirteen and a smart-ass. Nothing we said made him understand that this was not a game.

The third fine, twelve thousand dollars, was for a crushed soda can he'd stuffed in the bag after I'd inspected it and put it at the end of our driveway.

The fourth was for a glass bottle he must have pinched from a neighbor's glass bin and tossed into the trash on his way to school.

Another family meeting. This time, just me, Ginero, and Jean.

"Son, do you realize what my being put in prison will do to your mother?"

He shrugged.

Jean slapped his arm. "God damn it, Ginero! What the hell has gotten into you? Don't you understand you are about to send this entire family into poverty?"

"So?"

"So?" Jean repeated. "So? Is that how you want to live? Like those children who have no shoes? Like the refugees? Are you so spoiled you can't see how good you have it?"

He sneered at us and yelled, "You call this good? I get everything I want! The kids at school make fun of me for being a spoiled rich kid. They call me 'Ginero Dinero'! I never have to struggle for anything! I hate it! I'd rather be poor like everyone else!"

I received the fifth fine in the mailbox, for two more crushed soda cans. Along with the bill for twenty thousand dollars, which was three months' salary, was a letter from the Rochester sheriff explaining the procedure for taking me to prison or one of the mining colonies, which would happen the next time we failed to recycle.

Jean hugged me in bed that night and swore up and down that she'd testify that it was Ginero's fault. That Ginero should be sent away, not me. But he was thirteen. And he was our son. She couldn't send him to prison any more than I could.

For three weeks, Jean and I would sift through every little bit of garbage in the garage on Tuesday nights. We'd re-bag it, put it in the bins and I'd lock the new padlock we put on the garage door to keep Ginero out.

On Wednesday mornings, I'd stand with the cans until the trucks and inspectors came, making sure Ginero didn't drop anything in on his way to school. It was at those times, while guarding my waste bins from my own son, I got angry about the whole mess. Part of me wanted to stand back behind the oak tree in the lawn and catch Ginero in the act, and then beat him senseless, like my father had done to me on a few occasions to teach me how the real world worked. Another part of me asked, if his behavior was, in some way, my fault.

It was a ball of tinfoil that sent me to H-125. He'd wrapped a paper towel around it and when Jean and I went through the trash that fourth Tuesday night, we just didn't think to unwrap the thing.

Not a day goes by up here when I don't think of Jean and the kids. Even Ginero, the little bastard. He'd be twenty-seven now. I wonder how they made it, if they stayed together or if my arrest ripped the family apart. I wonder if Jean is still as beautiful as she was when I first met her at the little diner two miles from the Niagara River. I wonder can she still afford to fill the hummingbird feeders and sit and wait for them to come and stick their long tongues in and drink the sugary water. I hope she never had to be hungry.

My walk home from River 16 takes me through Hermes Sector, where I can see the docking station for the biannual round trip to Earth. Today, the ship has come with three hundred new prisoners, each dressed in a color-coded thermal jumpsuit to designate his crime. In red are the white-collar polluters, CEOs of dirty corporations who get sent to the depths of the mineshafts to do the most dangerous work. In green are the litterbugs, whether a gum wrapper from a car window or a transport trailer full of scrap or garbage, who go to work in the civil service. In yellow are personal-use criminals like FR (Failure to Recycle), water wasting, sewer violations, or OEL (Over Energy Limits) who get sent to the mines to become human trains, like I did, to move the tons of slag with their bare backs.

The arrival of the ship means in two weeks, there will be a departing flight, with three hundred lucky lottery winners on it, which means a week from today will be my last lottery.

At an intersection, a transport bus stops to let opposing traffic through, and I look at the men, who gaze in shades of awe, out at their first dead planet. Are they disappointed by the endless gray? The lack of clouds and wildlife? The cold from a too-distant sun?

Suddenly I am looking at Ginero, who is looking back at me. We lock eyes for two seconds before the transport jerks him toward whatever quadrant his mine will be in. He raises a red-suited arm to acknowledge me and I say, "Wait," but the bus is gone, turned round a corner and out of sight before I register that my son is on H-125. A slave.

I run after the bus, hoping it might stop, hoping I was wrong, that it wasn't him, hoping that I can rescue him, but it accelerates and I stop, wheezing, and realize I do not want to save Ginero. I realize I want Ginero to save me.

> > >

A week later, on payday, they announce three hundred lottery winners. I'm not one of them. I ask my payment officer if transfers of Earth credits are allowed to H-125 prisoners. He tells me it's possible, if I pay the right people the right amount of credits.

"So, would five million be enough? Do you think? To get the job done?" I ask.

He grins. "I think that ought to do it, yeah."

"So what if an old man wanted to find someone here? Would an extra two million buy him a quadrant location?"

"That sounds reasonable," he says, looking over my shoulder at the line of men to be paid. "But the old man had better hurry up."

I hand him a slip of paper with Ginero's name on it, and after a quick tussle with the computer, he hands it back, with the address. I scribble it onto my palm, and slide the paper back to him, because he knows what to do next.

Can I trust him to only take seven for himself? No more than I can trust Ginero, if he ever gets off H-125, to take the money home and help our family. No matter. At least when my body is hooked and dragged from the river, I'll have lived for something up here in this wasteland. For now, I stare at the numbers on my palm and wonder what kind of man I will meet when I visit, and whether I will like him.

> > >

Ginero stares at me through the thick glass, and the lines on his forehead stretch wide with worry. I want to put him at ease and smile, but admit to myself that part of me wants to break through and strangle the thirteen-year-old boy he once was. I notice his manicured hands, and compare them to my splitting thumbs and my septic calluses and for a second I feel happy that he is here. Happy that he about to experience real work for the first time in his life...until I remember that he will be worked to death like the rest of us, and no matter what a boy does to his father, it is never a good thing to contemplate the death of your child.

We stare like this for a while, eyes darting from the floor to each other, to the other prisoners, until it is our turn to meet at one of the four visitor booths for our ten-minute conversation. When we are face to face, no glass between us, I see he still looks like Jean. Her chin, her eyes.

"Dad."

"Son."

He purses his lips, and frowns. "I'm so sorry."

I nod and squeeze my brow into the same frown. "How's your mother?"

"She's fine. Still lives in Rochester. Annie'll graduate school this year."

I feel hot tears run down my face. "Graduate? Annie?" I sigh. "How did Jean afford to stay in the house?"

"I don't know how she did it for the first years, but I got a job at the plant as soon as I turned sixteen and so did Darren."

"Darren. How is he?" The last time I saw Darren, he was ten, playing with plastic toy soldiers in the flower-beds Jean had just mulched. I can smell the spring air and the tree bark.

"He works in advertising. I stayed in the plant and worked my way up to the office jobs. Soon, I was bring-ing home as much money as you were before you got...sent...here."

"So you lived with Mom? Took my place?"

He nods. "Until I met Stephanie, yes. Then we moved into a place on Harvest Street. You know, near the park?"

God. The Harvest Street Park. The days I used to spend pushing Ginero's little denim-covered butt on those swings. The fun we had in the snow on the sliding boards. The time Darren slipped on the steps and split his lip.

"Stephanie? Is that your girlfriend?"

"My wife. We had a little girl three years ago."

I think about Annie when I left her. She was three as well. "I'm a grandfather?"

"Yes." Ginero is crying now, too. He wipes his eyes with his red sleeve. "We named her Jeanie, after Mom. She looks like her, too."

"Jeanie," I say. I can't hold back the sob. I am a grandfather. I pinch the bridge of my nose with my finger and thumb and then look at the timer. I have four more minutes.

"I miss them so much," he says.

"I know, son. I know you do. I guess you know by now that up here, they put out your candle once you hit fifty, right?"

Ginero suddenly looks at me, concerned.

"Well, if they haven't told you that, then I'm glad I'm the one that broke it to you. Up here, you aren't much use as an old man, and the fumes in the mines age you double anyway. But that's not why I'm telling you."

"Go on."

"Once you get free of the system, you'll get work, like I did, doing something else. And you stand to make a fortune doing it, too—a fortune you can't spend here," I say. "I made a fortune, but I'm never going to make it home."

"Oh, Dad."

"It's okay," I say, glancing at the timer. Ninety seconds left. "Look, Ginero. I transferred all of my money into your prisoner account. You won't be able to spend it up here, and you can't tell anyone about it, but if you're luckier than me, and you make it back to Earth, you can take it with you and give it to Jean and assure that our family never worries again."

He looks guilty. This secures my trust, and I smile and touch his hands. "You must tell your mother I love her, and your sister and brother, too."

"Will I see you again? Can't you come back and see me again?"

"Only once every six months, son. And in six months, I'll be floating down River 16, another lump for Frank to drag out and put on the conveyor."

"But," he begins to sob and grips my hand like he used to when he was a frightened boy.

"You'll make it, Gino. I know you will. Think of your wife and daughter often and you will serve your years here with purpose."

The buzzer sounds and we hug over the wide table. He is crying and I see his mother again, crying, having lost her husband and her son to this environmental tyranny. What sort of pitiless world divides a man from his young family for the sake of mere litter?

> > >

Walking through Hermes Sector on my way home, I see the launch pad and imagine Ginero flying home to his family. I see him at the bank on the corner of Elm and Green streets with Jean, transferring fifteen million dollars into her account. I see Annie going to college and becoming a doctor, like she wanted when I last saw her as a three-year-old, grasping her play stethoscope and laminated eye chart. I see Jean smiling a little, knowing I thought of them every last year of my life, knowing I loved them through all of my suffering.

I hug myself away from H-125's dismal horizon and imagine I am holding my granddaughter, my Jeanie. These are the things that give life meaning. Not numbers on a screen, or job security with hospital benefits. As I squeeze myself, I feel her squirm and nuzzle me with her soft, little-girl skin. I hear her giggle and squeal with ticklish laughter. I see her growing tall and broad-shouldered and I am happier than a man has ever been on this awful dusty rock.

I near G sector and begin to smell the river. I am happy to go to work today, to keep my mind from melancholy, to remind myself of the realities. But still, I have a granddaughter. This, somehow, makes the scent sweeter than it's ever been and though I know it must be my brain playing tricks, I remember the smell of a freshly washed child and baby powder. As I suit up, I breathe in baby oil and diaper cream. As I walk to my chest-deep platform in sector 3-C of River 16, I hear soft lullabies. As I hook a rusty old filing cabinet and motion to the crane man to pull it out, I feel, for the first time in fourteen years, like a proud father again.

HARRY'S GIANT

I hate when we lose. And I can never understand how the rest of the guys can tell jokes and goof around on the bus home. Seems to me they should be thinking about the mistakes they made, and trying to figure how not to make them again.

Take Lewis. He's the tackle who let those receivers through. He could have saved us the shame of fourteen points. The difference between getting beaten and whooped. Lewis has his earphones on, oblivious to this, he's smiling and rocking out, his bushy hair flopping back and forth with whatever heavy metal shit he's listening to. He's air guitaring and giving Jones wet willies with his spit-soaked finger, thinking this is all fun and games. All fun and games.

Lewis doesn't understand that my life depends on this shit. He lives in the burbs and has no idea where cheese comes from while I live five miles away, up at four every morning milking cows and feeding steer. Lewis doesn't want to get out of here. He's comfortable with the VW Jetta his parents gave him for his seventeenth birthday, and with his shag carpet basement bedroom. He's happy spending the checks he gets from part-time lifeguarding on new rims and that stupid German license plate he has on the front to make him seem like the rich kid he's not.

When we get back to the locker room, Lewis slaps me on the back of my neck.

"You hitting the diner, Fatboy?"

"Nah."

"Oh, come on!"

"I have to study, man. Big Calc test tomorrow."

But of course, that's a lie. I can't go to the diner because I can't gain any more weight. I can't eat anymore junk. No gravy and biscuits, no chocolate shakes, and no red velvet cake with butter cream frosting. My life is now ruled by protein shakes and Coach Byrd's diet.

He's a real nice guy to help me out like this. He meets me in the weight room before school four times a week and has made me see that my father's farm is not the only place on Earth. He talks to me about college and he's arranged a few scouts, too, to come see me play. God, I hope they're watching me and not nimrods like Lewis. No chance I'll get picked up if it's teamwork they're looking for with this bunch of morons.

> > >

"Harry, how much Hefa-Lak™ did you put into the feed yesterday? And did you dose the calves?"

It's three-fifty. In the morning. I was up until midnight studying Calc. I have no idea what I fed the herd yesterday. It's all a blank. I need to start writing this shit down.

"Yeah."

"Yeah what?" My father has a way of being confrontational early in the morning like no one else. He thinks that just because he's had to be up at this hour since he was ten years old, that we all have to act like it's normal.

"Yeah, I dosed the calves."

"But how much?"

"The cupful, like always," I say.

He nods and goes back to the milk room.

Ten minutes later, he's back. "It's time to give the girls their shots."

Dad treats them like daughters. Says if it weren't for the girls, we'd be broke and lost. I swear he loves them like human beings. When I was a kid, we'd name them, but now it's just number earrings, a box of room temperature syringes, and Probovac™, the growth hormone that's ruining my life.

We line them up and I clean the site, in the tailhead depression, those two little divots on either side of the tail, and Dad injects the stuff in there. We do it twice a month. He says it makes us money, so I shouldn't think about all the hogwash going around about how synthetic hormones can hurt people.

"Did you look in on Flossy?" he asks. Flossy is my Belgian Blue prize winner. We keep her in her own stable and feed her special pellets to keep her coat shiny.

"Yeah."

"How's she doing?"

I don't know why he's asking. He checks on her every morning, too. "Fine."

"She's due that calf any day now," he says.

"I know."

"Looks like a big one."

"True."

We did it by the book. The artificial insemination guy even double checked the stud for us because lately, they've been breeding heifers to get bigger stock, and sometimes, they don't survive calving. But something must have gone wrong because Flossy's calf is huge. She can barely walk now and the vet said last week that if she doesn't go on her own by Friday, he's coming out to induce her a month early.

"Harry, I want to warn you. I may have to cut her," he said.

I knew that. I mean, does he think I grew up here and haven't calved a hundred cows already? I knew.

> > >

Fourth quarter and it's still tied. I know the scout from Virginia Tech is out there, somewhere, with his little notebook, scribbling down facts. Fact one—I just blocked two sack attempts and took down their receiver. Fact two—I'm on a team with a bunch of idiots. Lewis is being lazy again

41

and our quarterback could have completed way more passes if he'd only throw to Harris, who's been pacing the end zone by himself for the last two downs. But the quarterback is a racist asshole and won't throw to Harris because Harris is black. Says he doesn't want to give him any stats. Why Coach even plays this guy is beyond me. There's a freshman quarterback who's just as good. But, of course, he's black, too.

Third down and Harris is still free in the end zone. The quarterback throws to King, though, who's got defense all over him, and it's an interception. Worse yet, I'm on the ground on top of two linemen, and Lewis gives up trying to catch the runner, so they score on the interception and beat us 37-30. Lewis is lucky this is a home game because if I had to put up with his bullshit on the away bus tonight, I'd probably kill him.

It's the most amazing thing I've ever seen. Flossy is cut down the side, all the way, and we've pulled the calf from her. It took four of us. Mom even had to come out to help. While the others go to wash up, I watch the vet stitch up her side, and marvel at the giant heifer calf. Flossy stares into space exhausted, and I realize that the scar means she will never win another ribbon. But the vet thinks it could be worse.

"She mightn't live, son."

"I'll look after her."

"She's pretty beat, Harry."

"I'll take care of her."

"Don't get your hopes up."

I mean, isn't that the mantra of my life? Isn't that what Coach says to us before every game? What the college scouts have said, so far?

Don't I hear it every morning I'm lifting weights with Byrd, running laps, trying to get this flab off, when it just keeps piling on? And in my head? "Don't get your hopes up, Fatboy. You were born this way, and you'll die this way."

The world just isn't fair. I'm eighteen. What did I do so far that I deserve this shit? I know what's going on. I heard our family doctor tell Mom all about it almost five years ago. Only Dad still makes us eat a 100% beef diet. Says we have to support our fellow farmers. And 100% beef means 100% *don't get your hopes up.*

Flossy is dead three days later. A mix of hemorrhage and exhaustion. There was just too much work her body had to do to heal from the ordeal. After they take her away in the truck, I clean out the stall and splash disinfectant around until the place smells like an orange grove. Then, I lay down new straw and heat it with the lamp, and take to mothering her calf. Poor thing.

She suckles so hard I have to plant my feet solid to balance the bottle, and I have to refill it twice. When I tell Dad this, he doesn't believe me.

The next morning she takes three. Three bottles. And she sucks the teat right off the third one and cries for more. I try to hug her, but she nudges me to the door. Clever girl—and just like Flossy. Her manner is familiar, insistent, and warm. Three days old and she's already the size of a calf of two months.

When the vet comes to check on her a week later, I'm standing by the stall door with a percentile chart. No amount of math classes have prepared me for charting the calf's weight. She's off the charts.

"She's got a case of bovine gigantism, Harry." That's what the vet says. Bovine gigantism. I'd never heard of that.

"She won't be a show girl, anyway." Not like Flossy, no. Not a show girl, unless you count freak shows. I've got the Andre the Giant of cows.

> > >

Lewis is throwing an end-of-season party and he's got

43

Deep Purple blaring and half the party has spilled into the backyard in the cold night where neighbors can see and hear them. I know it's stupid of me to expect maturity from this guy, but come on. He's out front jumping from car to car, trunk to roof to hood, leaving dents and not caring about it at all.

And what is there to celebrate? Our 1-16 season? The only reason we even won that one game is because the quarterback was injured and they put in the black kid, Freeze, and he and Harris ate up the field and made the rest of us look like leftovers.

"Hey! Get the fuck off my car, man!"

Lewis is jumping up and down on Harris's roof, playing the drum solo on an air drum kit. He doesn't hear him.

"*Hey*!" Harris says, snatching at Lewis's ankle. "Get the fuck off my car!"

It's his dad's car. Lewis knows it. Lewis thinks every kid should have his own car because he does. Told me once that people would like me more if I didn't drive my dad's old pickup everywhere. "And you could lose a few pounds. Nobody wants to be friends with a guy who has tits," he said.

Lewis is still jumping, so Harris yanks his leg out from under him and pulls him down from the car and on to the road. Then he starts beating the shit out of him. After a minute of face-smashing thuds, the neighbor comes out of his house with a cordless phone.

"I'm calling the cops!" he says, waving the phone.

Lewis and Harris can't hear him. Deep Purple is so loud that no one at the party can hear anything but Black Knight Live in Berlin. I want to help, but I think Harris will think I'm a racist asshole if I stop him beating Lewis's ass. Plus, I think Lewis could use a good ass-whooping. Maybe he'd grow up, then.

So I make my way to the truck and drive home. I figure the cops will come any minute and I don't feel like getting busted for shit I wasn't doing. Anyway, Byrd says I can't

44

ever have beer with my metabolism.

> > >

It's Saturday morning and I'm running around the track. Three miles wrapped in trash bags in the dark. Byrd says I'm doing great under the circumstances. He's pissed I can't lose the flab, though. It's coming off my waist and my butt, but not my chest. I can't tell him it's the hormones, but I know that's what it is. I'm not stupid. This morning before I came out here to run, I walked through the sheds, filled the feed troughs, smelled the antibiotics we give them now for increased mastitis, and had the same daydream I always have.

Harry's Daydream: Dad dies young and leaves the farm to me. I turn it into an organic dairy farm, allowing us to charge more for the product rather than dose the herd with unnatural crap that gives teenaged football players tits and causes their sisters to start their periods at age eight.

I used to have other daydreams. Back when I heard the doctor tell my mother about the other boys—four of them. Back when I still thought my dad was a hero.

Harry's Old Daydream #1: Dad realizes that dosing the herd is hurting human beings, including his own children, and he decides to turn the farm organic.

Harry's Old Daydream #2: Dad stops making us eat beef every night.

Harry's Old Daydream #3: Dad takes this all the way to Washington, D.C., and fights the companies who lobby to keep the hormones in use. He brings me as proof, and I don't care that he parades me in front of Congress, saying, "This is my boy. Look at him! He's got tits!" because it's for the greater good. Isn't that what parents are supposed to do? Protect their children? From drug dealers?

One day I'll escape. My college prospects don't look great now that the season is over and no scouts were interested. But I'll escape somehow. Become vegetarian. Cleanse this shit from my system and start over. But for today, I have work to do.

> > >

"Harry!" my mother yells. She doesn't come out here this early, usually. I'm immediately worried. I find her holding the front page of the paper, pointing. When I get close enough, she tells me that Lewis is dead, and it takes me a minute to register. *Lewis is dead?*

You mean Lewis, the bushy-haired blond Deep Purple loving asshole who ruined my scholarship prospects by being a lazy teammate? You mean the name-calling spoiled suburbanite Jetta-driving asshole who told everyone to call me Fatboy in the seventh grade? *That Lewis?*

Before I could read about it, there was a crash behind me and then, loud cattle racket. When I get to the shed, I see her, the giant calf, now the size of a yearling bullock at only six weeks old, running amok among the dairy herd. Again. This is the fifth time this month. She stops and gobbles on an udder, the cow kicks at her and freaks out, then she bucks and takes off. She jumps the gate and lands out in the field, thrashing her head from side to side. It takes my father an hour to lasso her back in. I have to fix the door with steel hinges and bang the bars back into shape.

"I'll need to call the vet, Harry," Dad says.

"For what?" I know for what.

"She's not right in the head, son."

"But can't we just keep her in a bigger stall? Maybe this is her way of telling us she needs more room. She's all I have left of Flossy." My mother would call this grasping at straws, but it's worth a try.

He sighs and sends me to the steer shed to clear out the back pen where we keep spare equipment. On the way out, I take the front page from where Mom left it, and tuck it under my arm. Before I begin the job of making Flossy's giant calf a new home, I sit and read about the death of James Lewis. Beaten to death on the road outside his house. Harris is in the County, locked up until a trial, and the

46

community is in shock. They call Lewis a football star. A local hero. I feel like throwing up.

"Are you okay?" Mom asks as I'm washing my hands before lunch.

"Yeah."

"You were close to James, weren't you?"

"I guess." *I guess, if you call that close.*

Just as I'm finishing a steak sandwich and a pint of milk, the phone rings. It's Jones and he tells me they're gonna lynch Harris's older brother tonight as revenge. And because I can't figure out what to say, and my mind is more on losing Flossy's calf, I don't say anything at all.

All I can think about as I'm hammering hinge pins in the high steel gate on the new stall is how screwed up this place is. On one hand, we all want to be Donovan McNabb or Emmitt Smith, and on the other hand, we're still talking about lynchings. I think about Lewis and how I'm never going to see him again. How if I'd have broken up the fight last night, he might still be here. How if I'd have that one extra ounce of courage and self esteem, which he helped whittle away with his decade of name-calling, I would have never left the party in such a cowardly hurry. What a mix-up. Before I can stop myself, I'm in the stall, sitting on the itchy fresh straw, crying about the whole irony of it.

Everything is wrong.

Everything is just plain wrong.

So I go in the house and call the police and tell them that Harris's brother is gonna get lynched and leave it to them to figure out what to do about it. Then, I find my mother, down in the laundry room, and ask her to make me an appointment with the doctor to finally talk about my options.

> > >

The anesthesiologist asks me to count from ten. I see him in his Snoopy character mask, preoccupied with the equipment and the gas he's regulating, and then suddenly he is

Lewis, and he is laughing at me. 'Fatboy got his tits cut off,' he says.

Then I'm in a rodeo where everyone has breasts. Even the kids. And the dogs. And the rodeo clowns swing theirs around in circles to make the audience laugh. I'm there to show Flossy's giant calf.

"Next up, Harry's Giant! A Guinness record holder folks! Look at the size of her!"

And when we walk out, her, the size of a two-story house and me, with breasts like Mae West, the crowd goes quiet. I knew she'd knock them dead. I am proud and I am feeling like a winner for the first time in my life until someone shouts, "Holy shit! Do you see the size of that kid's knockers?"

There I am with the world's biggest cow and the only thing the crowd sees are my breasts.

And then I wake up in the private room alone. A few hours after, my mother picks me up and takes me home to recover.

Two weeks later, I'm in the shed with Dad trying to figure if she'll grow more and if she does, how we'll keep her.

"Why don't we call her Babe?" Dad says, staring in at her.

My father likes his puns. A Belgian blue calf with bovine gigantism named Babe.

"Sure," I say.

We're silent for a few minutes.

"I'm proud of you, Harry. I think you made the right choice."

Which choice is he talking about? Calling the cops? Speaking at Lewis's funeral? Visiting Harris in jail? Naming the calf Babe?

Or is he talking about the breast reduction surgery?

Because if he is, I don't want to talk about it.

LEROY CAN TELL YOU WHEN

Leroy can count by seventeens without using his fingers. He can look at a crowd and tell you how many people are in it. He knows what x is before I finish reading him the equation. He knows about sin and cos and tan and all the buttons on my algebra calculator.

Thing is, he's too slow to know to be thankful. If I say, "Leroy, do you know how lucky you are to be a math whiz?" he says something like, "Thirteen words. Forty-one letters." If I say, "Can you help me with my math homework?" He says, "Always happy to help the retard." That's his favorite joke. And he laughs for about five minutes every time I let him crack it.

Today he's counting by twenty-twos. He says this will get him to a hundred thousand in about two hours. I don't doubt him.

There's a girl on the bus who Leroy likes. She's little and in kindergarten. He's ten and big for his age. I try to tell him not to talk to her in case she gets scared of him, but he won't listen.

"Hi," he says.

"Hi," she answers, spelling H-I in the air with her finger while she says it.

Then, she asks him to show her what's in his book bag and when he does, she asks for all of it and he gives it to her. His spelling homework, a SuperBall, his library book, a notepad he got in a Cheerios box, and a watermelon-shaped eraser. I bet if he had a million dollars in there, he'd give that to her, too.

Her mother meets her at the bus stop and has to wait

while she crams all Leroy's stuff into her backpack. I hear her every day asking, "Where'd you get all that stuff?" And the girl tells her that Leroy gave it to her.

That's fine until Leroy gives her his underpants.

The phone rings later that night, and it's the school. When Mom hangs up, she comes into the living room and grabs Leroy by the shoulder.

"Show me your underpants!" She grabs the waistband of his Lee jeans roughly and looks inside. "Where are they?"

"Mom, he—"

"Leroy, where are your underpants?"

"I love that girl," he says. "On the bus."

"Did you give them to her? Did she see your privacy?"

"Her name is Annie."

"Mom. He didn't mean anything bad by it."

She sits down in front of him, cross-legged. "Leroy you can't give people your underpants. They're part of your privates. Remember our talk about privates?"

"Seventeen words. Eighty-nine letters."

"Leroy, do you understand that you can't give away your underpants?"

"Yes, Mom. Eleven words, fifty-four letters."

"You can get in big trouble, you know?"

Mom is still in her white pantyhose. Her swollen red feet shine through and I can see she's still wrapping the corn on her right big toe. She sighs and goes back to the kitchen. She's making German sausage and mashed potatoes—Leroy's favorite.

Today, Annie isn't on the bus. During Social Studies class, the beige phone in Mrs. Dunkel's class rings and she tells me I have to go to the office. I strut to the hall, where worry hits me. What did Leroy do this time?

When I get to the office, Annie is there, sitting in one of the orange chairs, watching the janitor hang Christmas decorations in the hallway. I wave to the secretary and sit

50

down, and watch the janitor climb an old wooden ladder to string garland across the ceiling and staple it to the foam panels. Annie's right hand traces letters in the palm of her left, like a pretend notepad with one block capital letter per page. I follow her finger. A-R-T-A-T-T-A-C-K. Art Attack?

"John?" It's Mr. Killian, the principal.

When I get into his office, I see Leroy sitting there, with an icepack on his face.

"Leroy, what happened?"

He moves the ice to show me a swollen eye. "She hit me."

"She did? Why?"

"Her dad told her to."

I look at Mr. Killian. "So how is that his fault?"

"I want you to sit with your brother on the bus from now on."

I nod and the secretary beeps in. Mom is here.

When I look back at Leroy, he's counting again, with that look on his face like numbers are his only friends. That peaceful, glazed look that I wish I had instead of being worried all the time. I know it's bad to wish it, but I do. Sometimes I wish I didn't have to worry about anything but counting by twelve to infinity. Sometimes I wish I didn't have to take care of someone who doesn't know to be thankful about my taking care of them.

Leroy tells me that I have lived 4,430 days. It's only when he tells me I have 16,784 left to live that I get curious.

"Stop messing," I say.

"I'm not."

"You are. You don't really know how many days I have left."

"Sure I do. I know how many days everybody has left." He never lies.

"Everybody?"

"Mom has 3,890. Mr. Killian has 7,312. I have 362. Har-

51

ry, the kid with the big cow at the rodeo last summer, has 24,826. And Annie, the girl on the bus has 32,835. And Mrs.—"

"Hold on. You have 362?"

He nods.

"So what's going to happen to you next November?"

"I don't know," he says. "Don't tell Mom, okay?"

"I won't."

"I mean it," he says.

I reach for my calculator and I figure out that I am going to die when I'm fifty-eight. This seems reasonable. Mr. Killian walks back in with Mom and Annie, and Annie's mom, whose face looks like a cat that got smacked.

"John has agreed to sit with his brother on the bus from now on," Mr. Killian says.

"Hi, Leroy," Annie says.

The adults shush.

Leroy waves, still counting.

"Is there anything else?" Annie's mother says.

I whisper to Mom that Annie shouldn't ask for Leroy's stuff anymore.

"It would be helpful if Annie didn't ask Leroy for his things anymore."

The girl's mother tenses. "Are you saying that my daughter asked for your son's filthy underwear?"

Mom inhales to answer, but then Annie stands up.

"Sorry I hit you, Leroy," she says.

Leroy jumps up and grabs her and hugs her so tightly she squeals and then he looks her in the eyes and says, "Your mom is gonna die in 14,754 days."

And she answers, softly, "I know. She's going to get hit by a dump truck full of rocks."

The three adults look at each other and roll their eyes.

But I don't doubt it one bit.

> > >

Mom doesn't believe me at first, but I prove it to her. I take

Leroy around the old folks home where she works and get him to whisper the numbers in my ear and I write them down, seal them in an envelope, and tell her to open it two months later.

She does.

Now we're on the road twice a week.

We go from home to home, meeting people Leroy whispers the numbers to me, I write them down, and Mom sells the list to the administration. They want it because if they know when everybody's going to die, then they can run the place a lot smoother.

When I ask her how it feels to be the mom of a kid-genius like Leroy, she says, "It pays winter coats for you two." When I ask her what it's like to know she has ten years to live, she says, "It feels like shit." When she asks Leroy how long he has, he lies and tells her Annie's number, and she says, "Good to know you'll both outlive me." She means, *Good to know dragging you around like this isn't gonna kill you.*

The thing that really ticks me off is that neither of them seems happy. I mean, Leroy has a gift, you know? A real gift. He can really see into the future. But Mom just treats him like normal. Well, if you consider normal dragging your ten-year-old around like a freak show to make money off him. She tells him to tie his own shoes, fights with him over zipping his own coat. Tells him to wipe his own butt. Not like I think she should treat him like a prince or anything, but it would be nice if she said, "Leroy, I'm proud of you," or something that real mothers say to their real fortune teller sons.

And Leroy is more upset than relieved every time we take him out of school. You'd think he could at least be thankful for that.

"I miss Annie," he says.

"But you don't even see Annie anymore. She's in kindergarten."

"I miss her on the bus."

I'd been sitting with him since the underpants incident. "But you don't see her there, either."

"But we talk."

They do not talk. "Don't fib."

"We do. We talk with our brains. She told me she likes my shoes."

"Good."

"I can tell you When, and she can tell you How."

"How she likes your shoes?"

"No, retard," he says, slugging my arm. "How you're going to die."

Leroy looks pretty much normal from the outside, but when he gets really happy, his face deforms a little bit. His mouth smiles like a special kid's mouth does—crooked and wet. He's looking at me that way now.

"I can tell you When and she can tell you How."

"So, How?"

"How what?"

"How am I going to die?"

"I don't know. Annie can tell you. She told me."

"So how are you gonna die, then?" The school janitor pops into my head. HEART ATTACK, not Art Attack.

"I can't tell you."

I grab him in that brotherly wrestling hold, like we're joking around. "Tell me!"

"Nope."

I wrestle him and pin his strong shoulders. With my face above his, I work up a big glob of spit. "Tell me or I'll let this drop!" He doesn't, so I let it drop slowly, and it snakes right up his nose until he coughs.

"Mom!" He wiggles free and I chase him down the hallway.

"What's so bad about it? Why can't you tell me?"

When I pry the lock open to our room, he's on his bed rocking, and I hug him and apologize. I try to crack jokes so he'll give me a goofy smile again, but he can't. He can only have one emotion at a time, Mom says. So, now he's

54

just sad, and so am I. Still, I wonder how he's going to die. And why he won't tell me. He tells me everything else.

> > >

The next fall, I'm in junior high, so I take a different bus.

"Annie's not coming to school anymore," Leroy says.

"Where is she?"

"I don't know. That kid Mark says she's dead, but I know he's lying. She still has 32,635 days left. I think she moved."

"That Mark kid is a jerk."

"He's only got 873 left, so I don't care."

"And how many are you down to now?" I didn't ask all summer.

"62."

"That's like two months."

"Yep."

"And you still won't tell me what Annie said? About How?"

"Eleven words, forty-three letters."

"Why not? You know I can take it."

Leroy puts his hands over his ears and starts to walk away. "Eight words, twenty-three letters."

My life has become so weird that I'm not processing this like I should. I have two months left with my little brother. That should make me do something other than mark the day on the calendar with an X.

I decide to give Leroy every spare minute until he dies. I get Mom to take us cool places, usually on the way back from a nursing home. We stop at a few harvest fairs and eat funnel cake. Leroy wins a six-foot long furry snake and refuses to unwrap it from his neck for a week. At nights, we play endless games of Transformers or checkers or backgammon, Leroy's favorite. I've been trying to track down Annie, too, because I can't stop thinking about How I'm going to die. Knowing When isn't enough. And Leroy would die happier if he saw her one last time.

"So, if you know How then can't you stop it from happening?" I ask, one night, over a bowl of popcorn and a game of Uno.

"That wouldn't be right."

"But what's the point, then?"

"What's the point of what?"

"Of knowing How?

He shrugs. "Uno."

"So in a month, you're just going to happily walk into the arms of death, with no urge to save yourself?"

"Twenty-one words, eighty letters. I don't know what you mean."

"You don't want to live?"

He stops and looks at me with his head cocked. He has lived a life full of acceptance. "Uno."

"So, in a month, you'll just do whatever it is that you know is going to kill you?"

"Twenty-nine days. Uno."

"I'll miss you, you know?"

This is the first time Leroy has ever seen me cry. He has no idea what to do. So he starts counting by forty-sevens to the tune of the Transformers TV show theme song.

> > >

Everything is going great, like normal, and then Leroy starts to freak out. There are still about forty old people left to see in the B wing of Harmony Hills main building. We brought the puppy today, for the residents to pet and scratch. Mom tries to divert attention by taking the puppy and making a big fuss over it. I am stuck with trying to calm Leroy down. He's never done this before. I take him to the men's room.

He sits on the tall, handicapped toilet seat and bawls into his fists. There's snot everywhere. He's drooling. Finally, he says something.

"I don't want to do it anymore. It makes me sad."

"Okay, Leroy. I'll take you home," I say.

"Mom wants me to finish. I can't finish!"

"You don't have to. I'll get her to start the car." Five days left, and Leroy shouldn't have to suffer like this. I tell Leroy to stay in the bathroom and I find Mom and ask her to get ready to leave.

"He has to finish this job, John." She squints at me.

"He's just a kid! He wants to go home!"

"Tell him he can go home once his work is finished."

Next thing I know, I'm helping Leroy slide out the small bathroom window. We get out to the parking lot on the busy suburban corner, and I take Mom's keys from my coat pocket and start the car. How hard can it be? Gas pedal, brake pedal.

And then I hear Leroy yell, "Annie!" and before I can stop him, he's running into stopped traffic at the intersection, and opening a car door. He's hugging her and she's squealing with joy until her father gets out of the car, slugs Leroy, and grabs her from his arms. The lights turn green and rush hour horns beep in the lane behind Annie's dad's car. Leroy rubs his jaw and tells Annie he misses her. Her mother is trying to direct traffic behind her, and jabbering into a cell phone. Presumably 911. The father winds up again to hit him.

"Please! Stop!" I scream. I can't get there fast enough because the eastbound lanes are still on a green light.

"Leroy, watch out!" Annie yells.

But before any of us can do anything, Annie's dad punches Leroy so hard that he flies into the eastbound lane. And Leroy gets slammed by a tractor-trailer.

After he hits him, the truck skids sideways to a halt, traffic stops, and sirens start. Leroy lands on the gritty shoulder, face-down. Annie is the first to reach him and she throws her arms around him, and says, "Leroy? Leroy?"

I get there a few seconds after, and lift his bleeding head into my lap. Annie's crying so hard I want to adopt her.

Her father drags her back into their car, and he steers into the nursing home's parking lot, and parks next to Mom's car, which is still running. The ambulance and cops arrive. Leroy is in and out of consciousness and keeps patting my arm with his limp hand.

"I love you, buddy," I say, and he smiles.

"I lied."

"You lied?"

Mom arrives then, "Leroy! Baby!" She looks at me, "What happened?"

I give her the wait-finger and look back at him. "You lied?"

"Two words. Seven letters. I didn't want you to worry."

Mom barges in, "Leroy? Baby? Just hang on." But Leroy keeps eye contact with me.

"You mean it's today?" I ask.

> > >

At Leroy's funeral, Mom wails. I feel bad for not telling her because her guilt is so big, it's swallowed our whole town. "If only I wasn't working so hard," she says. "If only I had more time to play with him." But she had time and she knows it. She was just taking him for granted, same as I was until I found out.

Annie's father is in big trouble. I told the police everything that happened, and they think it's his fault. He comes to Leroy's funeral and he's brought Annie. At the end, when we all get to file past the closed, white coffin, Annie stops for a whole minute and talks to him through the wood. I see her writing with her fingertip on the painted wood, in big, invisible capital letters. She writes, "HIT BY A TRUCK."

And I come to realize that I don't want to know How. I don't want to know When. I just want this day to be over so I can start learning how to live without him.

Which will probably never happen.

SKIN

1

It's wrong. Plain wrong and dumb. Ain't no hygiene involved. Ain't no reason to cut out the most exciting part of a boy's life like that. America got it all mixed up with their clean-cut ideas. Ain't nothin' wrong with a foreskin. Didn't God himself invent it?

I told Larry and he just laughed at me. "Aw, Jim. Don't let preacher hear you talkin' about this again."

"Well, why not? He done heard me on it before. I think it's right time we tell the folks in this town that they're doin' a disservice to the Lord. A disservice to their own boys."

"They don't want to hear about no dicks and fore-skins, Jim. They'll laugh at you as soon as you open your fool mouth. And preacher has plenty to worry about already with these elections comin'."

"No other country on God's Earth do this to their own, Larry. Anyway, I bet you'd take yours back if you could git it," I said, kicking dirt. Larry told me once that after Betty had the twins, he done never touched her again. Said he couldn't feel a thing. Course, we make blame on the women and their stretched insides, but it ain't all them, is it?

Sure, you go ahead and tell 'em about those poor girls in Africa. Oh that'll rile 'em up, make 'em go door to door and collect everythin' they can get their hands on. They might even make a picket sign or two, or start a letter writin' campaign. But they don't see the wrong thing they're doing here to their own 'cause some big britches doctor tells 'em that it's a mandatory medical procedure. Like God let every boy be born un-right.

How are these small-minded hicks supposed to know any better than what their doctors tell 'em? I never knew nothin' till I went and saw the world.

2

When our little Jimmy was born, me and Georgia had a giant ruckus over this idea I got. Course, she won. She looked at his little penis like it was a dead fish—like it was road-kill or pig's balls or somethin'. The woman made a face like she'd just ate limes. She said, "Jim, I don't care what you say, it just ain't *right.*" Now, tell me. How come us Americans got it mixed up in our heads like this? Thinkin' what a thing looks like is most important?

"Anyway, Jim, what's he gonna think when he looks at yours? Ain't he gonna wonder why his is different?"

"Hell no, Georgie," I said. "When he gets old enough, I'll tell him he got the better part of the bargain." She shook her head like I was talkin' about the sex alone. Like I was some fiend. Well, let her think it. She asks me questions all the time.

Why do men think so backward?

Why they drive so fast?

Why they beat their wives?

Why they touch little ones? Why they rape? Why they kill?

And I'll tell you again. You know what my answer is.

You can't sell every damn thing in the world with sex, and then cut off the best part of a man who can't afford to buy nothin'.

3

I was fixin' to go and see our Jimmy at the County when preacher called to the house. He looked humble and sad about somethin' so I sat back and sighed. What more bad news could the man bring us in a year?

"Georgia," he nodded. "Jim."

"Preacha."

"I got news 'bout Jimmy you ain't gonna like."

"He ain't comin' home, is he?"

Preacher shook his head. "He's with the Lord now."

Jimmy started by robbing the local gas station when he was sixteen. He got twenty-seven dollars and three packs of cigarettes. We was poor. He wanted things. He wanted everythin'. I tried to teach him 'bout the world, you know, and how there was more to it than the commercials on the television, and do you know what he said? He said, "Pop, you don't know shit." So I gave him a hidin' and sent him on to preacher. Course, he never made it to the parsonage because he saw the O'Keefe girl walkin', and when she wouldn't go with him, he hit her and, well, you know the story from there. Poor Mother O'Keefe still in black, mourning nine months on.

Georgia hasn't touched me since, sayin' how a boy is a reflection of his father. She know I ain't like that. She know I'm a God-fearin', God-lovin' man. She married me in 1970, fresh from two years in Asia, a good son and a good soldier. She know I ain't nothin' like Jimmy.

Once, after they sent him off to prison she asked, "Jim? You think Jimmy did that 'cause of somethin' *we* did?"

I couldn't tell her what I really thought. I said no.

"Then why, Jim? I thought I raised him to be a good boy."

"You did, Georgie. We both did the best we could. Can't blame it on nothin'. Just the way things go sometime."

4

Some folks will blame it on the television or violent movies. Some say Jimmy's generation is morally long-gone because of them ol' video games. But why would my boy kill? Takes a deep thing to kill. I know. I done it myself. Ain't no one thing can make you do it. Ain't no one thing made him do it neither.

Problem is, the world moves too fast. Ain't nobody gonna listen to my complaint without addin' one or two of their own. And before you know it, there's a mile of bitchin', and mine don't have any authority. They treat me like I'm a stupid man. Even Georgia, my own wife. They done changed the way they raise girls, but never changed the way they raise boys. And they sell everything with sex. And they cut off the best part of a boy before he even cry the first time. Then they ask all their questions without thinkin', when the answers is starin' them right in the face.

RAUL SHOWS ME THINGS

Here's the deal. Tommy Gretz had no idea that my mother is a slut, so how was he supposed to react when she grabbed his shoulder-length curly hair and planted her tongue so far down his throat he nearly gagged?

Of course she's drunk. Poor Tommy came back from the bathroom beet-red and perplexed. He didn't say a word, but I could tell she'd been all over him because he sat nervously on the edge of my bed as if we hadn't just been dry-humping each other for the last hour and a half.

"Let's smoke a joint," I say.

"Yeah."

I open the window and turn the desk fan toward the outside world, which is really the next door neighbor's kitchen. This means Mrs. Persinski will smell it and tell her geek-jock daughter a hundred more times not to hang out with me. Like no shit, Sherlock. No one wants to hang out with the drunk divorcee-slut's daughter. I've been unpopular since the fourth grade when she let me go to school in a blue sequined boob tube, a mini skirt, and wedge heels explaining to the other kids why it's important to bring an umbrella and a squirt gun to *The Rocky Horror Picture Show*.

Tommy is relaxing now. I put my hand on his crotch and he flinches a little. God. I hope my mother doesn't manage to get there before I do. I've been trying to break Tommy in for three weeks, and I'm dying to tell Heather what his dick is like.

Heather's been dating Kevin Platt for two years and they have sex all the time. She actually got a picture to show us. He's huge. Or at least the picture makes him look huge. I told her that next time he passes out with a hard-on she should put something next to it for perspective, like how they put quarters or rulers in pictures of jewelry or Indian artifacts.

"Did you study for Geometry tomorrow?" Tommy asks.

"Yeah. Just the theorems. I didn't actually do the problems yet."

"Me neither."

"Want me to show you?"

He coughs and smoke comes racing out of his nose.

Three minutes later, I'm teaching him the new theorems and we're messing around with our protractors, when the knock comes.

"Renee, will you come out here?"

"In a minute."

"Now, please."

I spray the air with perfume and eat three Tic Tacs for effect. She's standing with her arms crossed in the hallway.

"I thought I told you the next time you had pot in the house to share it with me? What gives?"

> > >

So, she tells me on my wedding day that Gerry had sex with her in the downstairs bathroom once. Said they were both drunk and it was before we were engaged. I mean, really. I'm standing here in my wedding dress, five minutes from walking down the aisle and she comes out with this. What else can I do but shrug?

"Go up and get seated, Mom."

"You don't hate me?"

"Of course not. Just go. I'll see you later."

Now it's just me and Heather. She's my maid of honor.

"Was she serious?" Heather asks.

"No doubt."

"God. I'd kill my mother if she fucked Kevin."

"Let's not talk about it."

But I have to admit, ten minutes later as I walk up the aisle and see Gerry grinning at me, I wonder if he thinks I'm stupid enough not to know.

> > >

We're driving ninety miles per hour through the 110-degree desert with the top down. Gerry has some crazy heavy metal shit blaring on the stereo and I'm still a little drunk from last night's bender, which included my eating the worm.

The trunk is full of dope for my mother. Her new boyfriend Kyle is a local supplier and he pays us five grand per trip to pick up out near Reno and drive it back east. Gerry brings a ton of speed with him and likes to race against his best time, which so far has been two days and seven hours.

Ninety is slow for Gerry. I think he's still hungover, too.

Two years married and we're still crazy in love. As far as I know, neither of us has fucked anyone else.

When we get back to Kyle's house, a ten thousand square foot place in the hills north of my hometown, they set us up in the back wing, closest to the kidney-shaped pool.

> > >

Two weeks later, we're all coming to the end of a binge. Gerry hasn't stopped giggling in days. Mom and Kyle have set up a badminton net and we all meet in the afternoons to whack the birdie into the air and watch it float down again. No one ever manages a volley. Kyle tries twice to kiss me in the pool, but I tell him that I've only got eyes for Gerry.

He laughs. "Gerry? Ain't he the resident toy boy?"

"Toy boy?"

"And ain't you the same as your mother? A little vixen?"

Enter Raul. He's about six-four with a waxed, curled moustache and wearing a black matador costume with embroidered thorny rose vines. He's standing in the pool and is completely dry. I can't figure out if he's real or not. Seems I've got so good at hallucinating that even I can't tell the difference anymore.

He speaks to me in Spanish and I answer him, even though I don't know a word of what we're saying outside of my two useless years of high school Spanish class.

"¿Dónde está Gerry?" he asks.

"No sé."

"¿No sabe?"

"No."

Then he points toward the pool room door where I find Gerry banging Kyle's sister on the green felt.

He points to the TV room where my Aunt Ursula is giving Gerry head.

In the kitchen, my slut of a mother is bent over the breakfast bar.

Raul tells me these things are in the past, but knowing them is for the best. Sometimes he shows me my future, too. Like today, he showed me in prison.

> > >

Meeting Tommy Gretz at the gas station is the thing that saves me. He sees me and smiles. I'm as high as the moon, so I don't do anything until he comes over to me, a box of Rice-A-Roni and two red onions in his hands.

"Renee?"

"Yeah?"

"Remember me? It's Tommy. Tommy Gretz?"

Tommy Gretz. The kid my mother finally managed to seduce after eight long months. Tommy Gretz—my first home porno movie. Tommy Gretz—the first boy I ever really loved.

"Oh, yeah. Tommy. Wow. You look great."

"Yoga." He nods. "Mind body spirit, you know?"

"Uh huh."

I get to the front of the line and order the daily-house-usual. "Can I have two packs of Salems, a box of Marlboro Reds, and four packs of Camel Lights?" Tommy raises his eyebrows. I reach for a pack of Big Red gum and throw it on the counter.

When I'm done paying, I turn to him. "Bye, man. Nice seeing ya."

Only when I get into my car do I see that he dropped his stuff on the counter and followed me out. He's standing by the driver's door, making the "roll-down-your-window" gesture.

"I hope you don't take this the wrong way, but you look like hell."

"What other way can I take that?"

"Are you doing drugs?"

I don't answer.

"I can help. I've been where you are."

"You have?"

"If I take you somewhere to get clean, will you try?"

Part of me wants to burst out crying, to be honest. I'm twenty-four years old. My husband is the neighborhood toy boy, my mother is the neighborhood slut, and my life is a mess. I know this deep down, don't I? Just because I wanted life to be perfect, with a perfect mother and a perfect husband doesn't necessarily mean it's going to materialize, does it?

He holds my hand. "Renee, you were the first girl I ever loved. I can show you a way out. We can get far away from here and start over, I promise."

We?

Tommy Gretz. What is he doing promising me the world after so long? And what do I have to lose?

> > >

67

I'm thirty-three weeks pregnant with Tommy's baby. We're in Idaho on Dr. Adam's Farm, about fifty miles south of the Nez Perce Reservation. I haven't seen my mother or Gerry since the day I went out for cigarettes and never came back.

Tommy and I live in a round lumber cabin like everyone else here. There are a hundred of us, all ex-addicts, arranged in a circle around a six-acre communal garden and meditation area. Dr. Adam founded this place five years ago, sick of the government's half-assed way of dealing with its war on drugs (which he says is really a war on drug addicts). Tommy is one of the head counselors.

Dr. Adam visits me nearly every day and we talk about the life I would have had—full of drugs and prostitution. He put me in charge of the garden this summer and I try my best to keep him satisfied with my work. In my eyes, I was as much saved by Dr. Adam as I was by meditation and yoga, but I'd never tell him that. And really, it was Tommy who saved me.

Sabrina, the woman from three doors down, an ex-crack head, told me once that Dr. Adam fools around with all of the other women. I've never seen him with anyone but his wife, Evelyn, yet something in me feels that she's part-right. Adam only comes to visit when Tommy is away and everyone here is always pregnant.

> > >

We've just scheduled the baby's birthday. I'll have a C-section on August 16 in the local clinic where Dr. Adam knows a doctor who does them for cheap.

"Think of being pregnant as divine work, Renee. And get used to it," Dr. Adam says, hand on my belly after we finish some Hatha positions.

What does he mean *get used to it?*

His hand slips down to between my legs and I snap them closed.

I'm at the door now, and he scowls and says, "But we share here."

Enter Raul. Today in a callused brown leather suit, pegged legs, boots and a cowboy hat. He's smoking a short cigarette and has a handkerchief in his left hand. His moustache is longer this time, starched into spirals. He's standing, resting an elbow on Dr. Adam's shoulder. Of course Adam can't see him.

"¿Dónde está Tommy?"

"No sé."

He pinches his chin and shifts his face around, concentrating an unbelieving look at me.

"De verdad, no lo sé," I say. I really don't know where Tommy is.

Raul shows me Tommy on top of Evelyn in my bed.

On the floor.

On the rug by the wood burner.

On the porch.

On the bed again.

He shows me Tommy with Sabrina, from three doors down. With Methadone-Judith and Mary the Baltimore ex-cokehead. He shows me three little boys with different mothers who have Tommy's dimples and curly hair.

Raul looks disappointed that I could be so fucking stupid. As if I didn't already know the world is a freak show.

> > >

The only thoughts going through my head as I walk the dirt track north are baby-thoughts. Where am I going to have this baby? How am I going to have this baby? What am I going to do after I have this baby?

I sit on a rock to drink water and meditate, but I'm distracted by the sound of drums. I can see miles in every direction. Velvet-green hills cracked with the streams that feed the Clearwater River. As I walk to the basin of the valley, I hear something following me, but there is nothing. Each time I hear brush crackling behind me, I stop and look and though limbs are moving, no one is there.

The midday sun is gone by the time I reach the bottom and splash my face with the river. It's only knee deep here. Refreshing. I squat down to fill my water bottle and when I look up, I see Raul, standing motionless like a road sign, a huge sombrero brim pulled down to hide his face, pointing me through the brush.

"Aquí." Go here. "Sígame." Follow me.

As he walks, I follow, noting his long shadow stretching to our right. The shadow grows longer as our journey nears the sound of more drumming. Now I can't figure if it makes sense that Raul has a shadow. I can't figure if it's possible that I can walk in his shade and feel cool relief. And yet, it must be possible because it's happening. And really—is it any crazier than my life so far?

Raul leads me to a small shack where a wrinkled old woman is standing in the doorway. She smiles at me, and though her mouth doesn't move, I hear her saying, "Don't worry. Your baby will be fine. You are ready. You are safe."

I sit on a tree stump outside the shack and rest. Raul is gone. The woman sits close enough to me that I can smell her sun-scented black and silver hair and I reach out my hand and she takes and holds it. We are now companions.

Instantly, she is the mother I always wished I had.

There is water trickling down my legs. The last of it. We've been at this for hours. Lily Blackeagle tells me that I am about to give birth. We are walking circles in the grass beside the creek, her chanting something in mono-tone-Indian and me stopping every few minutes to hold onto the rough bark of the central tree and breathe through my contractions. We walk again.

Another sharp sensation from my lower back. My body presses my pelvis forward and I nearly collapse. Lily leads me to the tree again, tells me to hold on to the strong branch, and kneels in front of me.

"You push now. I will catch the baby."

Dr. Adam told me that childbirth was unnatural and too painful for modern women to endure, that our bodies are inadequate and imperfect. He told me that it was dangerous, like a disease. He told me that it could kill me. Lily is kneeling, still hum-chanting, and smiling at me. She has no doubts. I feel like God.

I had no agony. I am sore today, but not dead. My baby girl is perfect and bright-eyed. I named her Lily. I am surrounded by Lily Blackeagle's friends and family, who are having their annual powwow and celebrating every atom of life, including my own, even though I'm not a part of their community or culture. They invite me to the dances, but I stay in the small, log-built shack with the baby and I rest.

My mother, Kyle, and Gerry all got busted the summer my Lily was born. Since then, Gerry's managed to run off and no one's seen him, Kyle's become a late-blooming dental assistant and has held the same job for eight years, but my mother, sadly, has never managed to change. Presently, she's in the County for credit card fraud; she's been hooked on meth for the last three years.

"You look like shit, Mom." I hand the guard two cartons of Salems for her.

"I know it."

"Can't they send you somewhere to clean you out?"

"Who? The same bitches who sell me the stuff?" Funny she uses the word *sell*. What money does she have but her body in here? She thinks I don't know, but Raul shows me things.

"How's Lily?"

71

"Great. Soon done with tenth grade."

"Time goes fast, eh?"

"Yeah."

"She smoking weed?"

"Not that I can tell."

"Good."

"Yeah."

"Do you tell her about me?"

I want to ask her what she means. Does she mean do I tell her about how we used to do drugs together? How she used to screw my boyfriends? How she's in prison now?

"Nah. She's a teenager. She's not listening anyway."

Fact is, I haven't told Lily the truth yet. She asks me about my mother and I lie. I tell her that the last time I knew, my mother was taking off to the West Coast to start a new life. "She sounds so cool, Mom," she usually says. "I bet she wouldn't make such a big deal out of the stuff you're always ragging on."

It makes me feel bad to lie to her because I never wanted to lie to my kid. Of course, I bet we all want that, but it never happens quite the way we planned, does it? Same as I never planned to be visiting my mother in the County, bringing her cigarettes.

I don't know when I'll tell her the truth. I don't think any of us are ready for it yet. I'm still holding out for the day my mother becomes capable of being a real grandmother, I guess.

> > >

We are arguing again.

"Why do you always have to tell me what to do? I hate when you do that!"

"I'm your mother, that's why. And you have no idea how lucky you are that I give a shit."

Every morning is like this. She either misses the bus, forgets her backpack, or skips breakfast. I just want what's best for her and she just wants to drive me insane.

"Why can't you just lay off?"

"I don't want you to be late to school again."

"You can always drive me, can't you?"

"That's not the point."

"But you can. You do anyway, don't you?"

I don't know what to say. Lily thinks I'm a taxi. A free taxi.

"Starting today, no," I say. "I won't drive you. Starting today, you walk."

She stops teasing her hair. "Walk? Are you crazy?"

"No."

"But I could get kidnapped! It's over a mile to the school! I'll miss two whole classes!"

I shrug.

"But I can't miss Life Drawing! It's the only time I get to see Jason all day!"

"Well then, I suggest you get yourself in gear and make the bus, then." I look at the clock. She has about four minutes. "I put a Pop-Tart in your backpack. And I signed your Algebra homework."

She huffs and kicks the bathroom door closed. I hear the tap dance of speedy make-up application and when she emerges, I'm happy to see that today, she decided not to wear the eyeliner a quarter-inch thick on her lower lid. She walks briskly into the kitchen, grabs her backpack and a banana out of the fruit bowl, and storms toward the front door with a minute to spare.

"I bet your mother wasn't this much of a bitch," she says, right before the door slams. And strangely, this comment gives me a warm feeling rather than an urge to chase her and make her apologize.

One day. One day I'll tell her. One day we'll drive to the County and she can see what I'm not—what I might have been. And I won't expect her to say much on the drive home.

73

WILL DEIRDRE BEAT THE ODDS?

Deidre is in whiteface. This is strange because Deirdre hasn't been a clown since she left Gorman's Circus fifteen years ago. She scoops out an extra dab from the tub and paints it thickly around her right eye, edging as close to the lower lid as she can to hide the bruise Stephen gave her before he left for work.

In the supermarket, children point and squeal, "Mummy! Look! A clown!"

She wants to twist them, like balloons, into animals. Into geometric shapes. She wants to stomp on them and hear them pop.

He's a joiner now—works for the PVC window place down the road from the government pork farm where he used to work. He beat her less back then, with salty bacon fists made weak by whatever he downed at Denny's pub. That was before the debts grew monstrous and he started betting to make things better. As if it would. As if imagining Spain would change the drab Irish weather.

This morning he said, "Do you know how much we fucking *owe*, Deirdre?"

She'd only asked him for a fiver.

"Do you know how much it costs to fix your useless, ugly mouth?"

> > >

She stops at the newsagent for the local paper to search for work she can do that Stephen won't find out about. She leaves and looks both ways before stepping off the kerb, and sees him outside Harry Maher's Bookmakers on the corner, smoking a cigarette. It's half-past noon. He's gambling his lunch break again. The horses. The dogs. The football. He'd bet on raindrops if he could. He'd bet on children racing in the park. He's convinced it's the same as investing. He's convinced that one day, it will all pay off.

"Deirdre?"

She turns to see Margaret and her heart drops. Margaret Lamm, God help her now. Everyone will know if they didn't already.

Margaret opens her mouth to say something, but Deirdre steps into the van and waves a frantic goodbye, looking in a hurry. Looking busy. Looking like an emergency clown on her way to make someone happy.

Stephen sees the van and squints. He shoves the betting slips into his pocket, tosses his cigarette into the gutter, and spits.

When she gets home, she calls Dr. Bill, her dentist, and cancels her Monday appointment. He's already asked once about the bruises on her wrists. Can't get a root canal in whiteface. Impossible to fool someone who won't be fooled.

> > >

At dinner, she can see the silver scratch card dust all over his hands and under his nails. He always wins a few quid. Two or five or ten. Fifty, once, on Christmas Eve the year of the big storm. He says it's free money, so he buys more cards with it. Some days he can stand at the counter for an hour, scratching and winning crumbs, trading them for more crumbs until his pocket is empty and the folded losers sit in a pile in front of him. She reckons he must spend a hundred or more a week on cards. Then fifty twice a week on Lotto nights. Always the same numbers. His lucky numbers. His lucky numbers that never win.

"Is this supposed to be white sauce?" he asks.

"Yeah." She looks to her lap, hiding the bruise from him because it makes him angry that she bruises.

"It's fucking horrible, Deidre. Tastes like dirt."

"Sorry. Will I get you some brown sauce? That always—"

Before she can finish, he picks the plate up and slams it on the table upside-down, and pushes his chair out. "I'm going to the pub."

She calmly stabs a bit of gammon steak onto her fork, slides it through her mashed, dips it in the parsley white sauce, and quietly slips it into her mouth. She chews until he's out the door, then finds the strength to swallow. Only two molars left now, Dr. Bill has suggested that she think about becoming a vegetarian. He says it will do her the world of good. Says it's healthy.

Healthy.

The opposite of wanting to die, which is what she is.

> > >

Someone burns down Harry Maher's Bookmakers on the following Friday. Stephen slips into bed at four in the morning stinking of diesel and Deirdre curls into her pillow and thinks about how life would be without him. She thinks back to when they met.

Summer of 1989, Gorman's was still a decent name. The matinee would still draw a decent crowd. The Moroccan tent men still followed orders and didn't threaten to sue for more pay and better conditions. They did the work—set up, pulled down, ushered, drove, helped Frank Gorman with the generator when the wagons would go dark because too many performers were using their showers or hair dryers or space heaters. The life of one-night stands in towns no one ever heard of, moving on at three AM, lorries stuck in the mud of football pitches littered with candy floss and empty popcorn bags—the life of circus, as crazy as it was, was still decent.

76

Stephen had been looking for work to get him out of hometown trouble. He wanted to run away and become a performer. The only talent he had was brutality.

So they let him train camels.

Looking back, she sees his strong back, his bulging arms. She sees how charismatic he was, and how that first time, a small slap, was a clue she should have noted. But he was her rescue. She hadn't wanted to be Deirdre Big Feet all her life. She'd grown to hate the giggles of children, the look of awe on their faces when she'd squirt them in the face with the flower on her red, polka-dot lapel. She'd grown to hate their stupid, squeaky-voiced questions, their older brothers who would try to slice the guy ropes with their pocketknives. She'd had enough of making other people happy while she grew miserable.

The diesel smell turns her stomach. When she is sure he is asleep, she goes to the kitchen and picks up the telephone and places it on the table. She stares at it. She doesn't know he burned down Harry's, but what she does know is that Stephen owes Harry a lot of money, and he smells of diesel. What she does know is that Stephen has been stealing from the joinery to pay Harry a weekly bit. What she does know, since talking to Dr. Bill's receptionist yesterday to reschedule her root canal, is that Stephen got fired last week and still hasn't found a way to tell her.

"Who do you think you're calling this hour?" he barks from the doorway.

"What?" Before she can shake off her surprise, he has her by the hair.

"You want your old man locked up, eh?"

"Let go of me." She frees her hair from his menacing fist, "I wasn't calling anyone."

He walks out to the hall and digs something out of his coat pocket. He returns and slaps down a wad of pink Lotto tickets in front of her. "There's a winner in here. I can feel it."

There are a hundred or more.

"Jaysus! That's a week's wages!"

"*My* week's wages," he says. "*Mine*, Deirdre."

"But there's bills. I…I…need to buy food."

"Didn't you hear me?"

She crosses her arms and stares at him. He truly thinks they'll win. She can see it in his eyes. Innocent. The same as the idiot children believed her feet were really that big.

"We can't eat Lotto tickets," she says.

His face contorts. Before she can move, he grabs her hair at the scruff of her neck and crumples a handful of tickets and shoves them one by one into her mouth, leaving paper cuts on her lips and jarring her nose so hard with his fist, it bleeds. She can't breathe, and as she tries, he stuffs the tickets in harder, and she feels the inside of her mouth become dry. The ticket paper sticks. It's in her throat. It's in the spaces where her molars used to be.

"That'll teach you to keep your fucking mouth shut," he says, letting her weak head flop onto the cup-stained pine tabletop. He grabs up the rest of the tickets, storms out into the darkness of early Saturday morning and takes off down the gravel driveway, spinning angry wheels.

> > >

Harry Maher has told the police that Stephen burned down his place. After Sunday Mass, they question Deirdre about his whereabouts. She tells them every-thing—from the diesel smell to the fact that he didn't come home last night.

"He'll kill me," she says, showing them the yellow-green eye from last week, the paper cuts around her mouth, and her missing teeth.

They promise to lock him up once they find him and leave their phone number.

78

She locks the doors behind them and switches on the midday news and sits with a cup of tea and a thick slice of stale brown bread. She attempts to listen to the headline stories, but her brain is on automatic—trying to figure out an escape fifteen years late. She considers taking the ferry to see her sister in Bristol. She considers taking the bus north to find her younger brother, who last she heard was working for a bank in Dublin. She considers Gorman's Circus again. Eight months a year being dragged from mucky field to mucky field entertaining misbehaved, sugar-fed children.

The weather report comes on and snaps her out of her own thoughts.

Rain. Wind. Clouds.

She catches the recap. Protests at government buildings. Two murders in Dublin housing estate. A missing girl is found safe. Rain. Wind. Clouds. And someone won the Lotto last night, but hasn't come forward yet.

She's frozen as they rattle off the winners. 12, 16, 23, 34, 36, 39 and 25.

12, 16, 23, 34, 36, 39 and 25.

And then, she is in the kitchen bin, uncrumpling pink tickets still stiff with her spit until she finds it and double checks the numbers.

Triple checks. 12, 16, 23, 34, 36, 39 and 25.

She smoothes it, folds it, and tucks it safely into her bra cup, and walks down the hall to her bedroom. There, she inspects her hollow, molarless cheeks in the dusty mirror, packs a few clothes in an old carpet bag, and rings a taxi.

How I Became My Father

What it is, is a tree-lined street, a rainy night, and Ronnie's birthday. He's seven.

What it is, is that feeling I get when I think about that street. That night, the rain.

Someone says "dead as a doorknob," and that's when I start crying. Because this is my little brother. Because this is my dead little brother. Now is not the time to say things like "dead as a doorknob." Now is the time to push in his hard, cold tongue, dry him off, and find his church suit.

When it was just him and me here, I poked it a few times to try and get it to sit behind his bottom teeth. Have you ever touched a dead tongue? Have you ever felt the nothingness of what will never be said again? No more *Tag, you're it.* No more *Marco! Polo!* in the pond in the summers. The tongue won't stay where I push it. He is sitting up too straight. Until we lay him flat, it will taunt me by making him look retarded.

Dead, cold hand. Ronnie was my only brother. I was going to teach him everything. We were destined to go places together. We were destined to become something special. Together. What will I be now? What can I amount to after this night? When will this street be anything but the street he died on?

"Richard, go to your mother in the kitchen."

"I want to help."

"Do as I say. Your mother needs you." My father says this in his tired voice. His two-jobs-for-no-pay-always-tired voice. I know a sliver of him is thinking this means one less mouth to feed. But who would know what he thinks? I think he's spoken to me three times in my eight years. And I've only ever heard him order Mama around and tell her to get her head out of her pill bottle.

What it is, is knowing I'm the only one left for her to cry on.

How I made up my mind right then to get out of there forever.

Those people behind me, fallen leaves slick on a street I would never see again.

On his fortieth birthday, I bought Ronnie his own 126-foot Oceanfast yacht and docked at the Tokyo Club next to ours. Nadia always complains about our neighbors, no matter where we moor. This way, I can have control over half of them, anyway, because half the neighbors are now my long-dead brother who Nadia cannot complain about.

"Gosh. I wonder who owns *that*," she says, acting like I don't know what she's saying. "How long do you think it is? Longer than ours?" Give her time, she always, eventually, says it straight. "I bet it's a hundred and twenty feet long, Rich! Gosh! Imagine how much it *cost*!" With Nadia, this is all that matters. The boat could be full of rotten tuna or dead, smuggled refugees, but how much did you *pay* for it?

> > >

Back in the office, I am picking lint from the sleeve of my autumn-leaf-brown Armani suit, listening through the bad connection. Someone is telling me that my father is ill. It's my cousin Jack. My cousin Jack who I haven't talked to since the rainy night thirty-three years ago. Jack who said, "Dead as a doorknob" like it was my hamster that died. Jack, who never had any brothers to lose.

He's telling me who's there at the old house. Something about saying goodbye.

"Not much time left."

"Thanks for letting me know, Jack," I say, and press the button on the phone. I dial one for Dahlia, my assistant.

"Dahlia, send my mother some flowers, will you?"

"Yes, sir."

"Just sign *Richard* on the card."

Richard, the one who got away from you. The one who is never coming back. The one who married up, who keeps a home in five cities, who travels the world in his hundred-foot yacht, the one who has made it to Somebody, whether that damned street meant it for him or not.

> > >

Milan, two weeks later. Dahlia patches through a call from his mobile phone, bedside.

"If you want to see him before he dies, you'd want to leave now and pack light," Jack says. I tell him to send my father my love. He starts to say something, but I switch back to the conference call about Fresh Energy Corp.—the IPO stock we're either about to dump or not dump. I tell Dahlia, "No more interruptions."

Nadia is due from Japan in three days. She said she had some "final shopping" to do before flying south. As if she'll never shop again.

> > >

For Ronnie's forty-first birthday I bought him a sixty-two foot 2005 Sunreef sailboat for cruising the Med. I docked it at Y.C. Italiano, Genova, next to the one I bought Nadia. I picture myself slugging him in the arm, grinning, asking him how two boys from Welfare Street ended up here. I picture us anchored, lying on deck, cloud busting the Mediterranean sky.

> > >

My father's funeral is a blur. I was drunk for most of it. Nadia hadn't made it back in time from Tokyo. And then she stayed an extra week rather than in Milan without me. I found the whole maneuver odd, but I don't question anymore. She's all too quick to explain how *her people* do things.

82

"Funerals. Ugh!" she sighed, like she was talking about a plastic plate of shelter food. I wanted to remind her about *her* father's funeral, as if he was the King of fucking Spain, but it occurred to me that I didn't want her there anyway. She's completely useless.

What it is, is the fact that I married my mother. But instead of an over-medicated cleanaholic who was too busy to take Ronnie to the hospital after I pulled him out of the pond, I got an over-dressed shopaholic who is too busy to help me through my father's funeral. A nagaholic who doesn't want to have kids because they seem like too much work and they'll deform her body.

What it is, is the fact that I have become my father. Absent. For whatever reason. Even though I thought my life was the complete opposite of his.

I didn't go back to the house after the burial. I told my driver to arrange the fastest flight back to Italy, which meant I was on a plane, tucked into two cozy duvets with champagne and three Amedei truffles in hand before I ever sobered from the morning's events. When I woke above the Atlantic seven hours later, I'd managed to block everything out but the now-posthumous hate I have for him.

Nadia is radiant, grabbing at me from across the deck. We've been out for six hours and already, she's bored. Seeing my mother makes me want to try harder to be a good husband.

"I want to go back."

"But you said you'd spend the night," I plead, adjusting a sail rope.

"I know, but I just remembered about that boutique sale. I should call Luca and make an appointment."

"But we were supposed to...you know...christen it."

"Richard! We already had a party! And plenty of champagne! Now, I just want to get back on dry land. I think I might be feeling seasick." She regards me over her Gucci sunglasses and smirks.

I am leaning forward, hands on my knees, the sun in my eyes. I'm squinting at her radiance. I'm realizing that I'm forty-two years old and I hate my life.

In court, she acts as if every penny we have in the bank is from "Daddy." This is beyond annoying because Nadia couldn't stand the old prick ever since he beat her gay brother unconscious in 1986. As if it isn't annoying enough that I have to prove I'm a self-made man outside of her inheritance and back up my entire existence with reams of paper, now she's beatifying her black-hearted bastard of an old man.

During closing arguments, her lawyer stands up and produces two poster-size photographs, mounted on foam core. One of the ivy-covered mansion she grew up in, and one of my low-income childhood street. It was like getting stabbed, seeing it again.

He says, "Surely if things were *reversed* and *he* came from *here*," he holds up the mansion picture, "we'd all be certain that the girl who came from *here*," he holds up the white projects picture, "was a gold digger out for his money.

"I hope, esteemed jury, you will remember not to stoop to sexism."

Everything was muffled after that. I could feel Ronnie sitting beside me, holding my hand. I could see us in the glossy picture, cloud busting in the ragged backyard. What does it matter what I'm left with now? What she takes?

What it is, is realizing that street is everything I'll ever need. Ever want.

What it is, is the feeling that I get when I think about next week, when Ronnie will take me for a spin on the Oceanfast, out in Tokyo Bay. How we'll marvel at Rainbow Bridge. How we'll swim together, deep, how instead of me pulling him out this time, he'll pull me in.

BUTCHER

I have cut off my ass and sent it to you, in a box marked
FRAGILE! THIS SIDE UP! Now, my jeans fit. But I can't sit
down. Because I have nothing to sit on but raw bone.
Coccyx. Pelvis. Femur.

When you open the box, you will see the usual meat—
blood, globs of yellow fat, veins, skin, strings of muscle
that once propelled me through the world on foot. Strong
gluteus maxima that used to walk, run, skip. Used to do
cartwheels. Fuck. Make you dinner.

"Debra, how did you get so skinny so fast?" the girls
will ask at the supermarket. And I'll tell them—I sliced
the fucken thing off and sent it to that asshole of an ex-
husband.

I'll show them the ragged gash, the scab the size and
shape of Nebraska. And they'll say, "Me, too! Me next!"
"Can you fit me in on Tuesday?" They'll all want to be
like me. Assless. A size ten again. A walking wound that
pees standing up into a cup because it stings any other
way.

I have removed every hair from my body and stuffed it
in there, too. The bushy eyebrows you hated to the nest
of thinned gray straw that nearly died keeping up with
whatever hairstyle you said normal women had. The
blonde of the 70s. The perms of the 80s. The straightening
of the 90s. I took off all the pubic hair you said I
shouldn't have. As if it was your option. As if I was a
rubber doll you bought, the day they were out of the
hairless ones.

"It's disgusting," you said, when really, it's disgusting

that you want to screw what looked like a little girl. That's what you see behind your eyes, isn't it? That's why every woman you ever married needed her parents' consent, right?

"It's normal!" you balked. "Look at the *movies*, Debra! All women look like that! You're a freak."

Me with my human ass and my human hair. Freak.

"Debra, where are your eyebrows?" the girls will ask over eleven-o-clock break. "Are you okay?" They will squint at my hair and know it's a wig. They will think I have cancer.

The backs of my arms, I've sliced them and laid them in the taped shoebox to the right marked, "Too Flabby!" Now I will maneuver like a rusted robot, my triceps and elbow joints sacrificed. And don't I look grand? Not like the night you told me that normal women didn't have arms like this. Remember that?

It was July, so I wore a sleeveless dress and you said it on my way out the door, "Jesus! You're not gonna show them in public, are ya?"

I was twenty-one and under a hundred pounds already from your size-four fetish. My sister asked me why I was crying and I told her what you said. She looked shocked, but not surprised. Everyone knew you were a prick before I did.

"How are you going to stock shelves?" Frank, the manager, will ask. He'll threaten to fire me again, like he did that time I got the flu and nearly died. Like the time I took off work to nurse you after your gallstones and found you in bed with what's-her-name you divorced me for.

The girls will marvel. "Look at how slender it makes you! I wish I could wear tight sleeves again!" I will show them my tear-shaped scars and tell how they itch.

Of course, this package would not be complete without my breasts. I have put each one, nipple-side-up, in the two mini jam jars to keep them round.

I can still hear you saying, "But the girls at the club have round ones!"

I told you they were fake—and you told me I was worthless. They fed our babies. They stayed their shape. Conical. Normal. Real. But now, you may have them. In the same little Ball jars I used to make your marmalade in. If you want, you can spread them on your morning toast. You can serve them on the side and call them fried eggs again.

The girls will be convinced I have breast cancer, especially since I took the hair off first. They'll comment about how slim I look now. How the sheer weight of breast tissue is a burden to the scale at our age. How they wish to be rid of theirs. Martha will say, "Mine are so long it's like a roll of salami."

Frank will stop talking to me altogether, like he did when Hilda lost her ovaries. He'll only ask me to come into his office if he has a question about something tax-related and he'll tap his pen the whole time.

In a few days, he'll probably fire me. What good am I now?

I have sliced off my face and rolled it into a shopping bag for you, there, next to my arm flab in the shoebox. If you find yourself bored, you can make a list of how many different kinds of ugly you can see in it. (The girls will send me Get Well cards and flowers. Handwritten scrawl declaring, "Thinking of you!" or "Here's to a quick recovery!" but they won't visit.)

If you like, you can go back to counting every wrinkle, whisker, and clogged pore again, like you used to in the good old days. You might want to point out my nose, and those hairs inside, the ones you called "all wrong." Maybe you might stop and smack or pinch my lips roughly like you did a thousand times before. To make them puffy, you said, like the women in the magazines.

"Christsakes, Debra! Can't you at least pretend you're sexy and pout?"

Or, you can remove it from the bag, spread it on the floor and pounce on it, like that time you said, "It'll take more than makeup to make you look human." That was John's wedding. And you said that when you didn't even have to. Ten years divorced, that slip of a slut on your arm, wearing white, no less. You said it as an aside. A funny quip. I was fifteen feet away and I wasn't even talking to you—but you couldn't let it go.

Because my lawyer was right. You just couldn't help it. And you were so proud! Even in court! And you wondered why the judge gave me the house? It's not my fault you stood up and said, "But look at her! That's not what real women should look like! She's disgusting!"

News flash. I am as much of a real woman as your two wives since. What did you expect? That the girls from your dirty little magazines would hop off the page and become real? That we'd all stay seventeen? Get air-brushed? Plasticized? So a jerk like you could love us?

There will come a day, you know, when your hair falls out and your skin droops. You'll look at yourself in the mirror and realize that it will take more than Rohypnol and ecstasy to make the perfect chicks fall for you. The escort girls will make jokes behind your back. They will comment on your stale breath and how your dick won't get hard no matter how many of those blue pills you wash back with ginseng juice. Right then, when it hits you, dig out this box. And kiss my fat white ass. Because as stupid and cruel and ugly as you were, you were human, and I loved you.

THE TESTS I FAILED

NATIONAL RIFLE ASSOCIATION OF AMERICA
BASIC RIFLE TRAINING COURSE – FINAL
EXAMINATION - 1986

Question # 9
    The front end of the barrel is the:
        a. breech
        b. receiver
        c. muzzle

I am pointing the (c) muzzle at Mike Stanisklowski. I
have my reasons.

> > >

Six days ago, I got a big yellow envelope in the mail from
Neversink Summer Camp. I knew what it was.

Sarah,
    *Enclosed are your NRA patch and certificate for passing
Basic Riflery along with your final exam from the course.
Your final score was 15/20, which equals a 75% C grade. I
suggest revisiting questions 5, 6, 9, 12, and 13 and answer-
ing them correctly with the aid of your Marksman's Hand-
book.*
    Hope to see you next summer!
    Bob

Bob was a total dweeb. Drove a 1970 GMC, wore thick,
smoked glasses and listened to ELO. He was a stickler for
rules. He'd say, "I run a safe range. Anyone who steps out
of line can go back to the BB range with the babies."

I bet it killed him that I only got fifteen out of twenty. If I was still up there, he'd probably make me study a whole extra day just to get an A. I don't know how I fucked up so much, either. I totally know the answers.

> > >

Question # 5

The major difference between rifles and shotguns is found:

    a. in the safety features

    b. inside the barrel

    c. in the stock construction

    d. (d. in the way it will splatter Mike's body all over the back wall of his garage)

I find him in his garage, fixing his bike tire. The frame is upside-down, balanced on three stolen milk crates, and he can't see me coming through the spinning mess of spokes and reflectors.

"Hey, asshole," I say.

"Huh?" he manages, before he stands and backs up toward the rusted door that leads to the house. I've been through that door a million times. Mike's been my friend since I was a little kid. We used to play baseball in the summers at the playground behind our houses. We used to sip fifty-cent root beers on rainy days inside the big blue barn and make gimp lanyards and sock puppets.

"You're crazy. Put that thing down." He's stopped with his hand on the brass doorknob.

I don't put it down.

I want him to crawl (b) inside the barrel. I want him to see what's coming. I want him to see the pellets that are about to scatter his perverted ass all over his father's tool bench.

"Where the fuck did you get that?" he asks.

> > >

I got it from my father's gun cabinet. The one in the hall.

The one that has two locks.

He bought it down at Eck's Gun Barn last summer the same time as he bought my first .22. Told me I could have it when I turned fourteen, even though Mom hated the idea. Mom hates all of our ideas because Jenny, my fifteen-year-old sister, is a real girl and I'm the son my father always wanted. I mean, even though I'm his daughter.

Last weekend, after I came back from summer camp, he showed me the keys in the sock drawer.

"Just in case, Sarah. If you're ever here on your own and anything happens, now you know enough to protect yourself."

My father had no idea I got a C on my NRA exam. All he saw was the patch I sewed on my jean vest, the few shot-up targets I saved, and the wrinkled certificate that said I'd passed the course.

> > >

"You're crazy."

I knock off the safety. "Just shut up."

He does.

I've got the barrel pointed at him and I back toward the electric garage door, attempting to steady myself before I exhale and squeeze, just like Bob taught me.

"Why are you doing this, Sarah?"

> > >

Why am I doing this? Why am I doing this? Let's rewind to yesterday. Let's rewind to when I looked out the window of my air-conditioned living room and saw my sister Jenny stumbling down the sidewalk, like she was drunk. She fell twice. Her eyes were closed. Her face was stuck between a euphoric smile and a frightened sob. Her mouth was bleeding. When I helped her into the house and let her collapse onto the couch, I saw the scratches on her legs and thighs underneath her sun dress. I saw her underwear was missing.

"What happened?" I asked her.

"Nothing," she slurred.

"Where's your underwear?"

She was passing out. Her eyes rolled white.

I shook her. "Jenny! Where is your underwear?"

"Mike's."

"Mike's? You mean Mike Stanisklowski? *That* Mike?" I stared at her. "Did he do this to you?"

She nodded and passed out. I shook her. Nothing I did would wake her. It was two-thirty. My parents would be home from work at six.

> > >

Question #6

When you consider every gun loaded until you have personally proved otherwise, you are:

    a. acting like a sissy

    b. showing that you know the first rule of safety

    c. unnecessarily delaying your shooting

"You know why I'm doing it," I say.

I'm aiming right for his beady little date-rapist eyes. I am about to personally prove that this gun is loaded. I am done (b) showing that I know the first rule of safety.

"I thought we were friends," he says, reaching for something on the tool bench.

"Put your hands back up, Mike."

"You won't shoot me."

"Yes, I will." He's trying to test me. He's still reaching.

"I'm giving you to the count of three," I say. This is a mistake—I know it. A lot can happen in three seconds.

Question # 12

A round of ammunition is:

    a. a magazine full of cartridges

    b. a cartridge with a round-nosed bullet

    c. one complete cartridge

    d. (d. presently in Mike's head)

He spins and hits the garage door button with the side of his fist and the door begins to lower. It scares me so much I yank the trigger and *kapow* (c) one complete cartridge into Mike's stupid Polack, pervert head.

I am now falling backward with the jolt, and I land half of me inside the garage, half of me outside the garage. I hit my head so hard on the driveway that I knock myself out and the last thing I see is the door about five inches from crushing my ribcage.

> > >

Question #13

    After cleaning the gun:
- a. all metal parts should be coated heavily with grease
- b. rags should be placed in the muzzle to keep the moisture out
- c. all metal parts should be oiled lightly

I wake up on the same couch where Jenny was yesterday. I'm freezing even though she's covered me with a blanket. My head feels dizzy and I look at the clock. Three-thirty. I'm thirsty.

"Oh, thank God you're awake," she says.

"Jenny?"

"I don't know how to get it back into the cabinet."

"Did you carry me back here?"

She nods, hands me a glass of water, and says, "You hit your head pretty bad."

"Mike's...dead?"

"Is he?"

"I think so," I answer.

"Just tell me how to get that thing back into the cabinet before Dad gets home," she says, pointing to the gun like it's a skunk or a nuclear bomb.

"We'll have to clean it first."

"How do we do that?"

I take her into the study and clean the gun. I wipe the

butt, the action, the trigger. I clean the barrel thoroughly and (c) lightly oil the bluish-brown metal. I do this without talking to Jenny, who is sitting at Dad's desk, staring out the window down the long view of suburban back yards. When I look at her, face grown up now, matured in an instant, I know that I've lost a part of my sister that I'll never find again.

> > >

After dinner, the local cops start canvassing our pastel-sided neighborhood. Jenny and I say we want to play Monopoly in our room, but really we kneel on her bed watching Doug Holt and his partner go from door to door. Dad's known Doug since they were in school together.

I sneak out of the bedroom door and lie quietly on the soft hallway rug, eavesdropping.

"Two black kids in a rusty red Chrysler minivan," Doug says. "Four home invasions and a vehicle theft between two and four-thirty."

"We were at work all day."

"What about the girls?"

My dad gets up to call us, but Doug says, "Hold up, Jim. There's more you should know before the girls come down."

He tells them about Mike being dead. My mother emits a gasp, then a sob.

"Sarah will be devastated," she says. And it occurs to me that I am. I am devastated.

I never want to shoot another gun, never want to see another boy, never want to grow up or be a woman or get my period or pubic hair or boobs. I want to stop time. I go back into the bedroom and Jenny hugs me while I cry. I tell her everything I overheard and we make a pact. If God lets us get away with killing Mike Stanisklowski, then we will never think about it again.

"As if it never happened," Jenny says.

I nod my head. "I promise."

94

"We can't let it ruin our lives." She means the murder as much as the rape.

"I promise. It won't." And when I say that, I remember the article I read once—the statistic. One out of three. One out of three is too many. And now, Jenny is our one.

An hour later, the four of us are crowded together on the couch in the family room, watching the local news. I'm puffy-eyed and sniffly, and my mother comforts me by stroking my hair. Jenny is cold and quiet. Dad shakes his head, and wonders aloud, "Just who do these thugs think they are, coming into our neighborhood and hurting our kids?"

> > >

CONTEMPORARY LITERATURE – FINAL
EXAMINATION
SUMMER SEMESTER 1993

I'm failing my Contemporary Lit course because the professor is a malignant misogynist asshole. I hate him and I hate the stories he made us read, so I just stopped reading. I've been asked to review the five questions from our latest quiz, on Updike's "A&P" and Vonnegut's "Welcome to the Monkey House."

Updike's story is just boring. I've read it twice. It's about three girls in bathing suits and the guys at a grocery store who ogle them. Gross. The Vonnegut story I can't read at all. It's about a future world where rape is a benevolent act. I mean, that's just sick. I'd rather fail the class than read that shit.

And it brings up stuff I'm not supposed to think about after a decade of keeping my word to Jenny.

My band—me, Jester, Keith, and Johnny—decided that the only way to practice regularly was to move in together next month. Of course, we all have ulterior motives. Jester got kicked out of his dorm, Keith hates his roommate, and Johnny and I are hot for each other. They're like the brothers I never had. And they are also failing Contemporary Lit.

> > >

Question # 1

In A&P: What makes Stoksie say, "Oh Daddy, I feel so faint"?

    a. Gas fumes
    b. Hot summer sun at the nearby beach
    c. Girls in bathing suits
    d. Getting fired by Lengle

We're driving in Jester's van to pick up a new bass amp for Keith. I'm in the back, sitting on the wheel well, Keith is shotgun, and Johnny's lying on the twin-sized mattress on the floor next to me. We have a gig tonight at a kegger at GDI on Harris Street. GDI are the anti-frat guys who are just the same as frat guys.

"What do you guys think about the quiz we have to re-take on Monday?" I ask, yelling over Faith No More's cover of "War Pigs."

"I hear it's a beach party," Keith says to Jester.

"Chilly weather and (c) girls in bathing suits. What more can you ask for?"

"What quiz?" Johnny asks.

"Contemporary Lit."

"Fuck Contemporary Lit," Keith says, air-drumming.

"Yeah. Fuck it," Johnny says, sticking his head up between the front seats. "I have twenty-five of these little beauties. Make you forget all about that asshole and his quiz."

Keith looks back at the foil packet and grabs it before Johnny can pull them away. "How the fuck did you get these, man?"

He grins. "I have my sources."

"What are they?" I ask.

"Oh, nothing," Johnny says, slipping them back into his pocket. We flirt all the time. There's something about that ripped-up flannel shirt he always wears. I poke him and

96

tickle him until he jumps on me and pulls me down onto the mattress.

When I finally get my fingers into his pocket and pull out the pills, we're parked in front of Santo's Music Shop. I read the back. *Rohypnol 1mg.*

It's Rohypnol.

"What the fuck?" I yell, now way too loud since the music is off.

"What? You don't approve?" Keith laughs.

"That's sick shit, guys."

"Just makes things easier," he says, "For everybody."

Jester turns around and tells Johnny to get up. Keith opens the back doors and light strikes the foil as Johnny puts the pills back into his tartan flannel pocket.

"Don't be such a priss," Keith says. "You're driving around with Jester the Molester and you're shocked about this shit?"

> > >

Question # 6

In "Welcome to the Monkey House," Billy the Poet views the raping of Nancy McLuhan and other hostesses as a way to combat:

    a. Governments controlling sexual freedom
    b. Billy's impotence
    c. The fear of flying
    d. Fear of death in suicide parlors

"It's not as bad as you think," Johnny says about "Welcome to the Monkey House." "Vonnegut is a fucking genius, if you think about it."

"You're trying to tell me that a story about rape being good is genius? Come on. You're a guy. I'm a girl. You know what I mean."

"But it's not really about that, Sarah. You're not seeing it in context. It's about (a) governments controlling sexual freedom. All freedom, really. You should read it. You'll see what I mean."

We're walking around the brick lecture buildings, killing an hour between classes. For some reason I still trust Johnny, even though I know he scores Rohypnol for guys on campus. I'm not sure how I feel about Jester and Keith anymore, though. From the day of the GDI luau, they treat me different. I haven't been in the van since. Can't bear to think of what's happened on that mattress.

Question # 23

In "A&P," Sammy uses the phrase "the two smoothest scoops of vanilla I had ever known," to describe what?

    a. Buttocks
    b. Ice cream
    c. Clouds
    d. Breasts

After our philosophy class, Johnny invites me back to his dorm room. An hour of studying later, Johnny leans in close and kisses me. Before I know it, his hands are everywhere and it feels like everything I always wanted. His hands cup my (d) breasts and squeeze them. He runs his fingers inside the elastic rim of my panties and presses himself hard against my leg. His kisses are insistent and mature. It's times like this when I hate that I'm a virgin.

I'm not really sure what happened or how. I know he didn't drug me, and yet I feel unsure if that was date-rape or sex or what. He's sleeping now, and I'm tossing and turning, so I reach over to his desk and flip on the reading light. I grab the Contemporary Lit text, turn to the Vonnegut story, and read it.

And then, when I'm done reading, I feel just like Nancy in the story after she was held down by eight well-meaning people while Billy deflowered her. I feel humiliated. But I feel human.

> > >

Question #14

In "Welcome to the Monkey House" What does Nancy say when asked what it's like to be a virgin at age sixty-three?

    a. Chaste
    b. Proper
    c. Pointless
    d. Convenient for her job

Jenny brought Dad's truck to help me move. When she arrived, Johnny was still sleeping in my bed, and so they had an awkward introduction. Johnny naked, under a flannel sheet, and Jenny jumpy with busywork.

"So that's Johnny?" she asks, lugging two boxes of folders and paper.

"Um, yeah."

"Are you guys having safe sex?"

"Jenny!"

"I'm serious. You're my little sister. I care about shit like this."

"Yes," I say. "Anyway, we've only done it twice."

"And are you cool with it?"

"Yeah. Sure." Something tells me she knows what I mean. She knows how to read my voice, how to read the spaces between my words. Suddenly, having a sister is ten times more precious than it was yesterday. And having a boyfriend is ten times as (c) pointless.

With her, I feel like a real person. With him, I feel like one of the bathing suit girls from "A&P."

Question #13

In Vonnegut's story, what does The Monkey House represent?

    a. Freedom
    b. A craving for bananas
    c. Sexual depravity
    d. Animal-like behavior

The truck is packed. Johnny has gone to his dorm to finish up clearing out his room and Jenny and I drive to the new house. Jester is flopped on the dirty green couch drinking a beer at eleven in the morning. Keith is shooting pool in the front room, listening to Guns N' Roses.

"Pick a room, man," Jester says, slurring. "Johnny's fucking late, as usual. Stayed out all night again last night."

We haven't told them that we're together yet, but Jester says shit like this to imply that we are, and that he knows.

When Jenny and I get to the top of the stairs, I look down to see Keith sizing up her ass and I give him the finger.

"They seem nice enough," she says.

"Yeah."

The two rooms that are left are small and one of them smells like cat piss. Jenny gives me a painful smile and pats me on the shoulder. I decide to go back down the hall and see the bathroom. It's so filthy I can't think straight. Suddenly (a) freedom is looking less appealing than RAs and curfews and snobby chicks who hog the dorm showers.

"Let's go get some lunch," I say. Jenny nods and follows me back downstairs. I stop in the kitchen and look in the fridge. The guys have replaced the fridge light with a red bulb, and have stocked it with beer.

"Hey, Sarah," Jester yells. "Come here for a sec."

I tell Jenny I'll meet her at the truck and go back to the couch.

"Your sister is H-O-T hot, man. How long is she staying?"

Keith is standing in the doorway, holding his pool cue suggestively, and twitching his eyebrows. "Did you tell her we're an equal opportunity employer?" he asks.

"Oh, fuck off, both of you."

I know they're joking, but I still can't trust them. Johnny told me that he doesn't get them Rohypnol anymore, but I don't believe him. In fact, if it wasn't for the gigs we get on weekends, I don't think I'd hang out with any of them anymore.

"Just tell her that my door is always open, okay?" Jester slurs.

Only when I get into the truck do I see the sign that they tacked above the crooked front door. WELCOME TO THE MONKEY HOUSE—in dripping black paint on a rectangle of plywood. I decide right then to drive to my parents' house in the suburbs three hours away and never come back.

> > >

REAL LIFE, PARENTHOOD & BEYOND—SELF EXAMINATION
AUGUST 1999

After I quit college, I spent five years on the Appalachian Trail. Trying to escape my life, I guess. Trying to escape responsibility. Men. My past. More tests.

I went through all the AT hiker girl phases. I dread-locked my hair. Started doing yoga. I stopped shaving and showering. I went vegan for a while. Hung out with lesbians. Smoked some weed. Started knitting my own over-the-knee walking socks. Turned out, after all that, I ended up just like I always was. Just me. And for some reason, even though I didn't do anything in particular to help myself, I felt happy about being me for once.

That's when I met Dan.

Yesterday, I gave birth to our first child. A boy. Ethan.

> > >

I nurse him, remarking on his tiny fingers. I marvel the life that wasn't here only a day ago. One little life that some-how now dwarfs my own.

"He's so beautiful," Dan says.

"He is," I say, but rather than elation, I feel guilt.

Some years ago, I took a son away from another woman with my father's shotgun. (I remember Mrs. Stanisklowski used to make us homemade cookies and walnut brownies and wipe our chocolaty lips with wet paper towels when we were done. She'd bring us popcorn in a big red bowl with real melted butter while we listened to the Phillies game on the back porch.)

We change the baby, and I look at his tiny penis. How can this little thing turn into the world's most ubiquitous weapon? And what can I do to avoid it happening to him?

> > >

Jenny came to see us last week. She's working for the Rape Crisis Center in Albuquerque, and as a nutritionist, she specifically helps victims face and overcome their eating disorders. I serve fettuccini alfredo, her favorite.

"The thing I don't get," she says. "Is how nobody talks about it. I mean, women getting raped is so common it's almost considered normal now. Like chicken pox! So why don't we talk about it?"

Dan shrugs. He's pretending to be all fatherly and busy, but really he can't handle this subject.

"It's like a fucked-up feminine rite of passage. The world is sick," I say.

Later, after dinner, we're having a few beers and looking at the stars.

"Do you want to know what I think?" Dan says. He's tipsy and I tense, thinking he might say one of those stupid things he sometimes says.

Jenny nods.

"I think men have never recovered from the feminist movement. I think they over-reacted and got all fucked up and stopped knowing what to do with women. Not me. I mean, I don't care about that shit. But most guys."

"I think that's the tip of the iceberg, Dan," Jenny says.

He sighed. "I knew this guy in college, and he loved getting girls drunk and then forcing blow jobs on them," he says. "He'd come back from a night out and brag about it. No one ever had the balls to say something like, 'You asshole, what are you raping girls for?' I don't know why we didn't say something, but we didn't."

"He probably hasn't changed," Jenny says, "A lot of guys do that shit to their wives, you know."

"I could see it on the other guy's faces, too. They hated it as much as I did, but none of us ever talked about it. Not even when we were bitching about his other crap."

"I only wish I knew what caused it," I say, "so I can make sure Ethan understands boundaries."

"Just do the best you can, Sarah. I'm sure he'll turn out great. Dan's a great example," she answers. But really, none of us know how to prevent it because it's an epidemic now. Only no one outside of this deck is saying so.

> > >

The honeymoon is over. I bet that's what Dan thinks. All I did was ask him to not fall asleep after sex, and he freaked out like the Incredible Hulk. I didn't even say it bitchily. I wasn't angry or anything. I just asked him, while we were propped up in bed on a Sunday morning, Ethan snoozing in the cradle, the *New York Times* and coffee on our laps, if maybe he might stay up and snuggle a little, or talk.

I even complimented the sex first, although in all honesty, things are getting a little old at times, but I don't think it's anything we can't handle with a little communication. But the only communication Dan is capable of right now is either screaming the veins out on his neck or muttering in the bathroom to himself. Geez. If I knew it was going to be like this, I'd have never said anything.

Later, I try again, even softer.

"Honey, I really want you to know I wasn't criticizing you this morning. I just wanted to talk about—"

"Yeah, you wanted to talk about how I never do anything right. Last week, I forgot to take the trash out and left the ketchup on the counter. Now, I'm useless in bed!"

"Dan. I didn't say that. You know that's not how I feel," I say, reaching for his hand, but he pulls it away.

"Just leave me alone, Sarah. I need some time."

This is like taking a test that I didn't study for. I feel like running. Screaming. Crying. I feel like escaping all over again. I feel like calling the cops and turning myself in. Maybe life wouldn't be such a struggle without this awful secret.

From the deck I watch him flip through the channels on the TV. I see him fill a bowl with pretzels and crack open a beer. The frown lines between his eyes are deep. He's thinking hard about not thinking. He's trying his very best to stop all thoughts. To stop all words, breakthroughs, or ideas. He's trying hard to freeze himself right here, away from me, forevermore.

This is the next test. I realize that it's my job to stop him from freezing. That it's my job to pull him along with me because he doesn't know the way out. That it's my job to be strong because he's not made of steel, like the TV has been telling him to be since he could crawl.

> > >

I can't believe this is happening to me. I'm so embarrassed I feel like throwing up. The security guard is actually coming back with the manager.

"If you don't leave now, I'm going to call the police," the manager says. He's about thirty. No wedding band. No dress sense, either.

Ethan is suckling away, tucked into my arm, and my breast is barely showing. Dan is freaking out.

"We're not going anywhere. What kind of policy is this?"

The manager bangs his fingertips together. "It's mall policy. Just finish up there and John will show you out."

"Mall policy? Where does it say that?"

"A customer complained."

"Complained? About what?" Dan is purple. The vein on his neck is pounding.

"It's my job to make sure our customers are comfortable," the guy says.

"Well, I'm not," I say. I'm about as far from comfortable

104

as I can get.

I look up from the baby and stare at the guy. Behind him, the mall blinks and shimmers with Christmas joy, and this guy can't see the irony. Even Mary breastfed the baby Jesus, right? And what about the four sets of breasts staring at me right now from the Victoria's Secret store to our right? Are breasts okay if they're wrapped in pseudo-Santa suits? Red velvet and white fluff? Are they okay in black lace but not here, doing what they're made to do?

"So where do you suppose women should do this sort of thing, then?" Dan asks, as I try to speed feed the baby, my back to the argument.

"We have bathrooms."

And my mind reels at how fucked up our whole world is. There I was, since I was fourteen, looking for answers— looking for an answer about why men rape women, looking for an answer about how I could save Dan from himself, looking for an answer about how to save Ethan from all of it—and here it is. There is no answer. I can't cure society.

I am powerless, like I never studied.

Standing between an over-decorated silver and gold Christmas tree and a six-foot-two security guard, I decide I don't care anymore. I don't care if I fail. I mentally break every one of my number two pencils and shred my cheat sheets.

I wrap Ethan up in his fleece blanket and shove my sticky breast back into my bra. I look at the manager and slot him into place beneath me, and say, "Merry Christmas." Then I smile and take my family home.

ABOUT THE AUTHOR

A.S. King is the author of the highly acclaimed *Ask The Passengers, Everybody Sees The Ants*, a 2012 ALA Top Ten Book for Young Adults, and 2011 Michael L. Printz Honor Book *Please Ignore Vera Dietz*. She is also the author of the ALA Best Books for Young Adults *Dust Of 100 Dogs*, many published short stories, and the upcoming *Reality Boy*. After a decade living self-sufficiently and teaching literacy to adults in Ireland, she now lives in Pennsylvania with her husband and children. Find more at *www.as-king.com*.

Made in the USA
Lexington, KY
29 July 2017